# GOING FOR BROKE

PAUL LYONS

# GOING FOR BROKE

a novel

algonquin books
of chapel hill

• 1991

FIC

Published by
Algonquin Books of Chapel Hill
Post Office Box 2225
Chapel Hill, North Carolina 27515-2225
a division of
Workman Publishing Company, Inc.
708 Broadway
New York, New York 10003

Library of Congress Cataloging-in-
Publication Data

Lyons, Paul, 1958–
    Going for broke : a novel / Paul Lyons.
        p.   cm.
    ISBN 0-945575-45-9 : $17.95
    I. Title.
PS3562.Y4492G6   1991
813′.54—dc20                          90-49408
                                          CIP

First printing

10  9  8  7  6  5  4  3  2  1

For Hilary, with love

Alan, Lisa, Mark, Alison,
Tim, Uli, Tom, Bill K.:
thanks for your friendship
and counsel during the
writing of this book.

Robert, friend and editor,
I owe you again.

We lose—because we win—
Gamblers—recollecting which
Toss their dice again!
                    —*Emily Dickinson*


watching
        doubting
                wheeling
                        shining and pondering

before it stops
at some final crowning point

Any Thought utters a Dice Throw
                    —*Stéphane Mallarmé*

# GOING FOR BROKE

HERE WE
DANCE

# I

Two seats down from me in the pub in Folkestone where I wait for the ferry, a man has a vicious gash on his face that's sewn together with thick black thread whose ends knot in blackened stubble. The ferry won't leave for three hours. Outside, through a drumming rain, chalk cliffs grin ivory in the dark. From the ferry these cliffs will fade in an amber haze. The deck will pitch and heave in the dark, dividing waves. Cold spray will slip and roll in rivulets down my windbreaker.

The whole right side of the man's face is a puffed blue-purple, the tissue hardening cicatrix. When I lean his way I see right into the cut, which looks at least three inches long, and practically through his cheek and into his mouth. Like a crazy medical maneuver made to operate on the gums of someone who's had his jaw wired shut.

"What are you looking at?"

"That's a pretty wicked cut," I say.

"What's it to you?"

"Just a cut."

"That's right, asshole."

The man drinks slowly, winces when his lips touch the mug,

the wince passing through phases; obviously it hurts him to speak. Without the cut he'd be a reasonably handsome guy. He's wearing a red turtleneck sweater, a black peacoat, and one of those mariner's hats that looks either a hundred years before or after its time.

"Why asshole?" I ask.

Really I'd like to ask about his face. Whether he stiffed the bookie or someone with a few strings gone from his guitar just slashed him.

"I know your type," he says.

"What's my type?"

"You're just like all the other assholes in the world. Think that over."

When the door opens a rhomboid of blue light swings across the floor; dust rises. The cold air wraps my scalp, yesterday so monastically cropped I flinched at my reflection when Figaro swiveled the seat. Never say high and tight to a Bulgarian barber over fifty if you'll mind being shorn.

"If I'm such an asshole . . ." I say, and then, under my breath, "then why are you the one who could sip a drink without opening your mouth?"

"Did you say something, asshole?" he asks, cupping one ear, then turning to face me for the first time, his eyes blue disks of the outside light.

The bartender folds what looks like a racing form, ambles over, leans over the bar in the space between the man and me, and side-deals me a coaster. He's got a balding spot that looks like a patch of skin glued to his scalp and tufts of gray hair on the back of his head and neck. He looks from me to the man and then back to me.

"Get him another," I say. "Double house-whiskey for me. No rocks."

The man with the gash holds both hands around the mug of

Bass pushed in front of him like he's about to choke it. A pinball machine in the corner emits a teasy jingle.

"Go ahead, drink up," I say to the man.

"I knew you were an asshole," he says, lipping his glass.

"Sure, no problem," I say.

"And quit staring at my face before I break your fucking head."

The first ride from Calais takes me a few hours into France. I sit in the back of a truck, leaning against the wheel-well between hoes, buckets, sacks of nasty-tasting millet and flower seeds. We pass through pockets of colder air. Mists coil off black pools like coffee steam. I come to at the turnoff when the driver honks. When I walk around to shake he asks if I want to sleep on his farm. I tell him I feel like walking and he pumps my hand heartily, writes an address that I stick into the outside pocket of my canvas sack.

Soon I'm out in the country walking a long level stretch through dark shapes of tree stands, the stillness amazing. A clear, clean stillness that lets me hear my own heart.

My heart beats hard.

The booze wears off slowly, dissipating in stages, then vanishes, leaving just the predawn cold. My eyes adjust to the dark. The ribbon of road sharpens, distinct in the dim moonlight, bisecting braided grapefields.

When the sky starts to redden I'm nearing another small town. At first there's just a strip of pink behind the few scattered lights. Then the color dulls while the sky lightens and strong slants of sienna bleed over the fields.

I sit down on my sack, aware that I haven't eaten since the plane, suddenly exhausted and emptied, a tug at the back of one side of my throat. It would be good to cry. But now I couldn't if someone laid five-to-one odds. Like the point of dry heaves.

Though I couldn't stop myself in front of Julie.

She said this wasn't healthy (I agreed), said she felt bad for me (many thanks), wished she could help in some way (I could recommend some), suggested I see someone (a barber?).

Now that congested sense of having played the fool, of having acted the pathological asshole, of that itch to jump out of places, bite someone's nose, it all drains from me, leaving in the pre-dawn stillness an almost ridiculous clarity. I'm in France, out of school, out of the city, nobody's grapplings in me, about to step into whatever comes next, needing something next.

The next afternoon I press hard on a short run, rinse off in a frosty pond, eyed by goats, then wait by the road. A truck has dumped a load of rotten apples. I've had a morning lift from a Moroccan speaking an English all "k's" and "l's" who yelled at me, like if he spoke loud enough I'd understand. Then a ride from an enormous British woman whose monstrous German shepherd keeps slobbering on my face.

"Barkus don't bite," the woman says, a laugh rolling out of her. "But he'll sure enough lick your face, love. Don't open your mouth."

I cut myself wedges of apple, wipe the sticky rot off my hands. On either side of the road boulders break moss-green hills into planes, and beyond them rusty fields and distant am-putated, cauterized trees. The road runs on like stitching on a ruffled bedspread, ducking in and out of the folds of hills, pass-ing distant, crumbling viaducts. Cars sail along, fast, then slower as they climb and disappear into tunnels of poplars. In the late-afternoon sun, the apples smell slightly sickening but sweet.

Forty kilometers outside Avignon a faded blue Volkswagen sputters to a stop and I trot through the dust, squeeze into the back. The door slams shut and I scrunch against the cool window glass. Trees pick up speed and begin to blur. The driver wears a squarish beret, his dirty hair rubber-banded behind his head like wheat. Long metal earrings hang from his earlobes. He's missing a chunk of a wide upper lip imperfectly covered by a short, stubby mustache. The other man, who introduces himself as Claude, wears overalls and a heavily patched vest. His reddish beard is tucked into the top of his shirt. We drive through towns with high pitched roofs and cobblestone streets, the mirror rattling furiously, about to dangle from one loose screw, and stop in front of a café. Reddish light sprinkles through roadside poplars, checkering the road.

"*Café*," Claude says, holding his hand out in a mock tremble. He tells me in French that Jean needs it for his nerves, and cringes at my accent when I respond in halting French that I'm not in any hurry.

Inside, we sit at a wooden booth marred with initials around a vaguely reflective linoleum table. Jean and Claude order *café au lait*. The waiter stands over me, lumpy face twitching, until I order a *jus d'orange* and a *pain au chocolat*. Across from us, in a booth like our own, there are two girls, a redhead and a brunette, both with hair cropped short, bangs straight across their foreheads. A jukebox croons fifties America, something along the lines of the Coasters.

Cleaned up and smiling the girls might be Oklahoma-whole-some, bubblegum-chewing, high-strutting in the slightly exotic baton-twirling way wasted on corn-fed linebackers. But they slump, shoulderless as old drunks, only their fingers moving, slowly rising and falling, fingernails clicking on the linoleum, as if attached to the chords of music. A dust-swirled triangle of orange light slants over the table, illuminating a cheap metal lighter that rests in a Cinzano ashtray. Jean pokes me in the ribs and points to the girls with a cretinous look that suggests he's rightly done time.

"Eh?" he says, hand on my shoulder, his nostrils widening.

"Qu'est-ce que vous voulez?" I say, glancing sideways at his hand, which slides off my shoulder and slaps the table.

"Regardez."

The redhead picks up the lighter, turns it over in her hand. She flicks the lighter a few times, watching the flame flare yellow and then harden into an orange-blue tongue. The girl flicks the lighter again and runs the back of her hand across it, stroking the flame with affection until with deliberate slowness her arm goes stiff, and lowers mechanically like a jukebox arm until it stops, quivering above the flame. Held that extra second.

For an instant her eyes press shut.

Her arm relaxes and a distant smile curls contentment into her face, an almost surprised, strained smile. A black, pinkening wheal rises raw on her arm. She gazes at it, eyes brightening as if momentarily fascinated but quickly bored. She lifts her forearm slowly to her face, then rests it back on the table, opening and clenching her hand slowly. Then her head swivels lazily and finds me, her eyes sleepy, surprisingly free of pain, her lips slightly parted, her cheekbones tight and glistening against her skin, and her eyes register by a sudden widening that she knows I've been watching, staring, and I'm jolted in that moment when someone you've been eyeing turns your way. On subways your eyes dart off and then swivel back, startled again by the second look. But our eyes tangle at once; her gaze narrows, making my face flame. I'm locked, unable to turn away, tight at the groin.

"Eh," Jean says, his eyes depraved.

"Comment?" I say.

"C'est pas mal."

"Si tu veux," I say. "I suppose not."

The brunette looks over at me, following her friend's glance, then looks back at her friend, shrugs with a blank, incurious expression.

I look down at the horseshoe-shaped shadow of a bite mark, still slightly green and blue on my forearm, where an interior decorator bit me a few weeks ago at the Holiday Bar. There's one for that poet who said truth must be proved on our pulses. I'd had a brutal evening at the blackjack tables in Atlantis, that lost city by the sea resurrected by the New Jersey cranes. I bused back to the Port Authority, then cabbed to the Holiday. Around 2:00 A.M. two hefty women in their sixties entered the bar lugging a toboggan, their coats dusted with powder, one wearing a stocking cap with a pom-pom to her waist. The decorator smoked clove cigarettes. Her laugh sounded like a soprano machine gun. An alternating red and green neon light frosted her face. She had a damaged look that made me give pause. The bartender shook his head at me. The people around us were speaking real fast or speaking Spanish. She said, *You're kinda cute but your hair's too long.* I said, *I got a pair of scissors at home, cut it any way you like.* She looked at me funny. *What have you got to lose?* I whispered, and woke the next morning with a headache and memories of legs hairier than mine and us staggering along Broadway, knocking down trash cans and then groping through lewd acts on her gurgling waterbed. Hard orange light filtered through orange curtains. My clothes hung over a lamp. A sign facing the bed said CALM THYSELF. I crawled to the bathroom, done in pink and green, and found a note saying, HELP YOURSELF TO JUICE IN THE FRIDGE THEN LET YOURSELF OUT.

"You better get a tetanus shot," Fred, bartender and friend at the restaurant where I worked, said the next night. "Humans got more germs than dogs."

The redhead's eyes don't flinch; her eyes are hard, grayish in the dull café light, taunting. There's something at once daring, accusatory, threatening, inviting in them. If I were to lose Jean and Claude, pull up a seat with the girls, plunk my sack next to their table, hold my hand out, what would happen? I grip the booth to make myself sit still. The girl looks away from me. She picks up the lighter again, rolls it in her hand, flicks it—once, spark, twice, spark; then it flares, reaches a steady height, and then, moving her arm toward it and lowering she turns back slightly, as if to say, *Eh bébé, American man, whatever you think I'm thinking's all in your own sick mind. Tu es fou, bébé. And you can hold this lighter if it gets you off.* And I feel again that irrepressible cool lift and look away, down at their frayed cutoffs and dusty, shoeless feet, and when I look back the girl's eyes are playing with dull fascination over a new burn on her arm as if she's never noticed me. Two burns on her arm now, each a bright red circle. Orange-pink across the room. As if she's accidentally let her arm rest on the mouth of a tulip glass.

When Jean and Claude drop me on the far side of Avignon the sun's a tepid orange and the horizon layers of deepening indigo and purple. In the distance lights of a small city glow into the descending dark. I walk toward them, starting to get a road buzz and thrill and tremor, that sensitivity to every sound and shadow, a pleasing adrenaline, vague alarming premonitions waking, alerting the senses. The way in a dark alley you keep your good hand free.

Walking out along the darkening gray road, I see the brown-haired girl fingering the lighter. She picks it up, flicks it a few times, holds the flame steady. She moves the flame under her forearm, holds it. For moments she's elsewhere, encased in a haze of pain. Then she returns, her cat-green eyes playing over the burns. Claude and I sit silently at our table, not looking at each other, waiting for Jean to finish his third *café au lait*. The waiter lifts my empty glass; I shake my head without looking at him. Suddenly, I'm furious to do something, anything. Even to grab the lighter and burn my own arm. The girls compare handiwork, shooting our table an occasional look. Dark circular scars dot their arms. Raised wheals on skin that looks too milky, unhealthily white and soft. Jean and Claude don't seem to have noticed. Outside it's approaching night; no rain in the air. Soon I'll be looking for a field to crash in.

And as I walk the road, pace quickening, the night-edge sharpening, the brunette's arm lowers again, adding to those hard burn scars. And suddenly there's just a close-up of the flame tickling her skin liquid pink, skin layers dissolving away. Then Julie's face appears, an implosion of images and expressions dancing over each other like the afterimages of dice, cards, snifters, dealers on bathroom tiles after a casino night, a cluster-memory jam session: Julie sullen, Julie meditative, Julie furious, the vexatious green-blue of her eyes, her head to one side putting on her earrings, hair sliding over one shoulder exposing a slope of neck, the profusion of that long straight black hair, at one point nearly waist-length, candescent in disarray, dragging over my chest, obscuring parts of her, the deltas crinkling around her eyes when she comes across a passage in a book that delights her, her lips slightly parted as in amazement, surprise, delight. There's Julie steaming down the stairs into the House of Backgammon, whispering with barely contained aggravation, "Jason, aren't you coming?"

"Fruit Slice," I say. "What are you doing here?"

"Damn it, Jason. You said you'd be there by . . ."

"Okay, okay, okay, last game."

"I'll bet."

"How much?"

"Hey kid, hey kid, hey kid, man. Lemme borrow some of that Fruit Slice for half an hour," someone says, the words swallowed by a chorus of comment and hoarse laughter.

"Yeah, right," Julie says, puckering her lips at the bunch of them. "Dream on."

I'm settling up—always the argument of who owes who what—kicking in a few bucks for time and cognac. The Bulgarians babble away, hands in other's faces.

"Jesus, Jason, are you coming or what?"

"All right, already."

And we're dancing again, Julie and I, alone, the tapering shape of her, arms around each other, adagio tempo, *Sur le pont, d'Avignon*, waltzing in the woods, crunch of spruce-fir forest stuff underfoot, stars sharp, landscape silver-gray and ashy in moonlight—we're kissing up against hemlocks or leaning against the trunk of a giant blowdown, me lifting one of her legs around me, and that leg guiding me, heeling me on, her back shimmying upward against the moss-lined trunk, the other leg on toe and the sound of our breathing, arhythmical, against the stillness. Waltzing. *Sur le pont, d'Avignon.*

Walking in the city you never hear your feet.

A cool breeze blows gravel and strips of blown-out tire over the road. I find myself humming to the metronome of my feet, the words leaping from elementary school with Madame Fang who called my French passable but my behavior "extremely poor and undisciplined." *Sur le pont, d'Avignon. On y danse. On y danse.* Here we dance, or rather, there one dances, same difference, if we understand each other. White bridges and churches, palatial strongholds of popes and cardinals, and over the ramparts elfin figures capering. Here we dance. So springy. Dancing *toute la journée.* All of us sorry-ass eight-year-olds sitting straight in our ties and navy jackets with crests embroidered on them. And I walk, covering ground, quite alone, an hour out of Avignon, my feet starting to ache.

# 2

No statistical law says you ever have to get picked up hitching. It's a common fallacy to believe that because you're in distress you can depend on kindnesses from strangers. Especially abroad, where all the hitching signals and body language get utterly mixed up. One driver's *hello* is another's *fuck you*. Why shouldn't you get your cheek cut, or have your body trashed in a dumpster?

I've never wanted to believe in odds, Monte Carlo systems, though from backgammon to blackjack you've got to believe that there are moves beyond craziness and superstition, plays which in the sweep of many games make all the wrong plays infidel. You have to want to find those moves for the times when superstitious things like not changing lucky pants or not eating during a streak don't pan out.

"Do you want to believe that you are descended from a monkey?" a good Christian once asked me.

"It's not a question of what I want to believe," I said.

"Yes it is," he said.

And he may be right. I've seen Slav, the magnificent Bulgarian—all heart, no brains—collect for hours in the subterranean

House of Backgammon on Broadway and Seventy-fourth Street, mixing moves out of the Cide-Suey cookbook, violating all statistical theories or systems of rational hope, playing his checkers unconsciously, his dice on fire.

"Now you must to go in the movies," he yells, slapping one of Piano Man's checkers.

The kibbitzers shake their heads in disbelief, saying, "Slav, . . . you roll like . . . like . . . like Slav. There is no other way to say it."

"Why?" Yakov the mad chess master asks.

"And they say there's justice," Piano Man says, paying out.

"There is," Acer says. "Just isn't in here."

And the first time I went fishing with my stepfather, Tom, I prayed a mangled butterfly back to life in upstate New York. I was fifteen, walking in a field of high wild grass and mountain laurel; that butterfly's wings were twisted, white gluey insect blood all over its body. I sat beside the butterfly and untangled the wings. It hadn't moved. Then it quivered. Like a wind was tickling the busted wings. And I looked at it and concentrated on it and started saying *please please please fly away, please fly away you butterfly* and wasn't surprised when the butterfly raised up and then righted itself, and then fluttered off, black and orange against the swaying of the fields.

But willpower's got limitations. Tom told me about one Ismonus, chief groundskeeper of the Deerhearst Lodge and man of slogans—*the difficult we do today, the impossible takes a little longer*—a man who grabbed fistfuls of poison ivy and rubbed the tangled red-green leaves all over himself to prove the superiority of the will. And days later could be seen standing, motionless beneath a blossoming willow, his face a rash with a sad expression, doggedly fighting the urge to scratch.

•    •    •

A few mornings south and west of Avignon, the hard metal prodding of a Portuguese farmer's shotgun wakes me. My head rests directly under a wooden Christ, some local icon beaming a sad look down into my face. The farmer stands motionless with a grim absence of expression, gun lowered. Mist pours over the field and I'm stiff and soaked in my Hollofil sleeping bag. I stuff the bag and bungie cord it to my sack, trying not to seem in too much of a rush, my eye half on the farmer who is still frozen, watching. I smile, waving as I back away. When I reach the road I turn and see him poking around the Christ with his gun.

After a few short morning lifts and then a three-hour wait in hard sun I'm picked up by five schoolboys in a covered jeep. They're heading for a festival that will last one week. Alexandre speaks *a lethal Engleash*. They all study Engleash in the school. I must to join them, he says. After they will put me back into the road. He pops a beer, sticks it in my hand. A road bump jumps beer on my face. Another boy wipes my face with his shirt sleeve.

"Me Oscar, you Bobby Washington, okay Bobby?" he says.

I press the cold can against my forehead.

"Okay, thanks, Oscar," I say.

"Bobby-Bobby," another says. "I am called Tonk-Tonk."

"Tonk," I say, toasting can against can. "Tonk."

The beer has a metallic taste. Tonk chugs his and then sends the can skipping along the road behind us. A car behind us dodges and slows to get out of range. Tonk-Tonk's chest is concave, hair greasy black and plastered on his head, his body dirt-stained under what seems a shirt inexplicably fresh for the occasion. His look is quizzical and crazed, a mixture of surprise, fury, and discomfort, like he's been chopping habanero peppers all morning and accidentally scratched his ass. We bounce over an open field and wind up in front of a corral.

Immediately the boys strip off their shirts and jump into the ring, where there are about fifty year-old steers and twenty men, taking turns chasing. A short burly man darts about despite a limp, his heavy leather saddle pants flapping, arms windmilling to separate the herd. When one's shaken free he chases alongside, reaching one arm over the steer's body to grab flank and trying to seize hair with the other hand, when he gets a good grip bouncing alongside, jumping as it bucks, flouncing around with rapid jerks, the whole corral now yelling, *Antonio O valente, o grande, o maioral, vai! Antonio, agarra um! Antonio.*

Antonio the *valente* rides it for about a minute until he's shown mastery; then another man runs behind the steer, grabs its tail, and yanks from one side, its feet hop-sliding, mud-sucking, knees almost buckling. When it slows and trots, giving only sudden defeated dashes, the rest of the men jump its back, wrestling it to the ground, leaving only the head exposed, and a man with arms so big I expect to see toes at the end of them grabs the head by its small banana nubs and holds it down. A scrawny kid fetches the red-hot branding iron.

The smell of burnt skin reaches where I'm perched on the split-rail fence; the creature's eyes widen to white and froth bubbles from its mouth. Then the released steer springs up, shakes itself, and tear-snorts through the open door of the corral into a rocky field, scrambling through wildflowers, incongruous palms, a rusty combine, one mossy whale of a rock.

When the steers figure out that to be caught means to have a section of midriff made into an undercooked steak they resist wildly. Another man starts off, charges. He separates one from the pack, the steer threatening him with kicks and then catching him one in the chest. The man staggers, momentarily bewildered, and then, yelling wildly through coughs, he chases faster, finally getting a hand over its flank. For a minute he bounces alongside, and then he's tossed again, somersaulting, and comes up chasing. Then the steer pulls up and bucks; one hoof touches the man's mouth. The kick is too fast to seem powerful, almost a flick, but several teeth fly out and a side of the man's face is smudged with blood. The blow drops him to one knee, stuns him. He stanches the cut with his sleeve, kneeling and collecting himself, shaking his head clear. Then he gets up, wobbling, orienting himself, and takes off after the crazy-eyed, bucking steer. Several kids run into the corral hunting for the teeth, the men shooing them out of the ring.

After hours of brandings and buckings, Oscar starts waving me toward the ring, gesturing at me with lighthearted exaggeration. Big sweeping invitations, *Come, Bobby, come, Bobby. Come on, Bobby Washington.* Things are Portuguese enough. I shake my head, eye him like he's loco.

Alexandre trots up to where I'm sitting on the fence, Tonk-Tonk following him with a slight limp.

"You must to get one, Bobby Washington," Alexandre says, almost imploringly, as if pleading for both of our honors, the seriousness odd on his smooth young face. There's mud all over him and a trickle of blood from a slight cut on his forehead.

"Please, Bobby Washington."

"No, no, Bobby," Tonk-Tonk says, a transparent smirk on his face, poking me with a finger spindly but strong. "Is too much danger for you."

"What's he say?" I ask Alexandre, looking out at the steers huddled, pressing against the corral.

"Is too much danger for Bobby," Tonk-Tonk says, poking me again. I shove his finger aside, point at him.

"Please, Bobby," Alexandre says, an earnestness in his throat. "Please, Bobby. Go get one."

There's a sudden hush and I feel everybody looking at us. Several voices, obviously annoyed with the delay but playing along to get it over with, yell, *Agarra um touro, pega um, Bobby.*

"Too much danger," Tonk-Tonk sings to Alexandre, no longer looking at me.

"No," Alexandre says. "No for Bobby Washington."

Tonk-Tonk says something fast and angry to Alexandre, puts a ten-escudo note on the ground and slams a rock on it, then starts pointing back and forth between the bill and the steers, babbling ferociously.

Alexandre looks him over, reddening, absorbing the words like blows, and starts reaching into his own pocket. But I grab his hand and say no. I haven't changed money yet: the smallest bill I've got's a ten. Ten escudos equals what, about a buck?

"Oh my God," Acer would say, throwing up his hands. "Just how do you say sucker in Portuguese? Hardon, you've been snookered, man. How you gonna give ten to one on catching a bull that ain't even got horns, man, with your bare fucking hands?"

Acer is a short, filthy genius who writes term papers for kids at Columbia when he can't get chess or Scrabble action, and who I once saw pull a black glob, formerly a banana, out of his jacket pocket. Ate it without blinking. Christmas break junior year I'd hooked a chess sucker, and Acer fished around in my sack and found a paper I was working on and said I wasn't the cretin he'd thought I was, just a schmuck.

"Your Wittgenstein sucks."

"Just what's wrong with my . . ."

And Acer grins, tucks in his belly, goes to work on my paper, x-ing through passages, babbling countercommentaries, my pen waving in his hand as he drones on, punctuating his comments with obscenities. The Einstein among my idiot savant friends.

"How's your chess life?" Acer always asks when I enter the House of Backgammon.

"Not so good, Ace," I say.

"Hardon, that class-ass was better than you deserved and you blew it. That's all."

When Tonk-Tonk sees me pull the ten-dollar bill out of my pocket and place it on his bill under the rock, he looks like he doesn't know what I'm doing.

"Bobby Washington," Tonk-Tonk says, affecting shock. "My Bobby Washington."

"Okay, Bobby," Alexandre says, slapping me on the back.

"Okay," I say.

"Good, Bobby," Alexandre says, slapping me on the back. "Now you must to say, Bobby. 'Diga, I will capture a steer. Eu agarrar um touro.'"

"Eu agarrar um touro," I say. "I'll get one."

"Okay, Bobby. Wait. Tu és muito corajoso. Now, okay. Now you get one."

"Yes," I say.

"Yes," he says. "That's good, you good Bobby."

I take off my shirt, and conscious of being stared at, of my paleness, of being larger than them but softer and less agile, I leap into the ring, starting off after the herd. The sun's hard, the air cool on my skin. When the steers kick I shy instinctively, then start again after them, all the men laughing at my cautious reflexes, now trotting along behind me windmilling their arms at the herd and yelling me on. I grab some flank and the steer tosses me and I somersault out of control, like when you're laundered by a wave, and land headfirst in mud and bullshit with five grinning faces yelling, the men pushing and slapping my back, *Bobby Washington, vai, vai, Bobby*, all pointing at the steer and shoving me after it, *Vai, Bobby. Agarra um, Bobby.*

Then the insult of getting kicked around, indulged, made into a muddy comic interlude, starts flustering me. A light kick trips me and I land wrist deep in mud and come up squeezing a mud ball in my hand and winging it, the muck splatting against the steer's flank. The steer kicks mud back at me, bolts frantically. The men roar laughter now, several also burning mud balls at the steers, and I hear the people sitting on the fence howling with laughter and catch sight of little girls practically losing their balance on the fence gripping their ribs.

I chase angrily, feeling hot and sweaty and moving toward

dizziness, carelessness, my face flushed. I grab flank and slide off, hard-slapping the moving knots of muscle, and lunge again; a hoof slams my shoulder, sends me sprawling, another grazes my ribs, busting the skin, a deep bruise immediately showing. My sneakers make sucking sounds in the mud, turning my movements awkward and slow until my left ankle—still weak two years after some spiked clown stepped on it during a race—gets trapped in the muck. I feel a stab on the instep and take a step or two, flex it a few times, knowing there'll be swelling, and stoop to tighten the laces.

Bruised all over and smelling of shit, still mud-caked, we eat in a long hall. Pig, sausage, lamb in an oily stew and much *vinho verde*, slightly acidic, tart. We're served by old women, all wearing black, their faces seas of wrinkles, bodies gracefully fat and strong, skin rough like scabbed trees. When a dog appears in the doorway a tiny woman zips a stone at it. They keep filling my plate with the fatty meats and broth-softened carrots and potatoes. The men take turns getting up on the table to sing. When it's my turn, I mount the table and bow. Immediately someone puts a glass of the white wine in my hand and I chug it and it's filled again. I sing a couple of notes and they all start yelling and hammering on the table; the wood plates dance, the silverware rattles. I've got an outlawable voice, and always crimsoned during high school chorus when exposed by sudden lulls. After a few more bars the hall is silent. I sing "Swing Low, Sweet Chariot" and then a song from a high school performance of *Pirates of Penzance*. No one shouts for another song.

After the tables have been bused we sit in the long barn, several of the men playing harmonicas, passing a wickered bottle containing something not wine. Tonk-Tonk's got my ten-dollar bill safety-pinned to his now-besmudged shirt and keeps saying *Bobby, Bobby, good Bobby Washington* in an annoying falsetto. *Disgusting, man*, Acer would say. *Enough to make you quit gambling for two weeks*. Someone chucks a lantern, which explodes with a crash, and all of us sing different songs as loudly as we can, the cacophony making a kind of sense, our misshapen shadows dancing along the walls, the not-wine spilling and flaring to a thrown match, the table a blue sea of flaming shots in the dark, the liquor glow making the old men's faces grotesque, every face angular, scarred, distorted in some way: a nose askew, a slightly torn eye socket, a caved-in cheekbone leveled and hard beneath layers of dirt and sweat.

Then I'm in a beat-up jeep with Oscar and another boy, Ricardo, who's driving, bouncing us over the fields like we're in a bumper car at Playland, the headlights showing occasional, whitened trees that we narrowly miss as if he's trying to hit them but can't quite manage. Every time the car grazes a tree we both slap the dashboard and yell. Oscar's sound asleep, and after a half hour Ricardo gets out of the car, staggers a few paces, tries to grab a tree, and collapses. I lift him into the back of the truck and start the car, but sit there looking at the way the headlights knife into the darkness and wondering which way I should drive or if we should crash right there. Then Alexandre pulls up on a motorcycle, and we horse it and Ricardo into the jeep and drive off.

Later, a revived Oscar, Ricardo and I ride behind Alexandre on the motorcycle, barreling down a pitch-dark winding road, whooping the line between hilarity and despair. At first I get flashes of us sideslipping, rolling and sliding, road-rash raspberries, the scintillations of scraping metal, us flouncing, following the crushed bike and flaming parts down a cliff. Through the booze haze, the night accelerates, picks up edge and zooms out over the dark spaces. My gut drops away at every dip of the bike. Alexandre just gathers it in on the narrow curves, banking the bike as low to the road as he can, all of us leaning in, dark heaps of sand or scrap metal, sudden lights looming up and rushing past, our headlights making the back of a parked truck ignite like sunstruck mica. Then the three of us in back are waving our hands and fingers side to side in the air like Baptists on the turns, screaming exaggerated yells as we swerve out over dark overhangs, staying on by gravity and the grip of legs, going where . . . and why?

We stop by a building with a flagpole in front of it, and Ricardo starts pointing at the flag and yelling at the others. It takes a few minutes to recover my legs; the road seems to speed forward like a motorized treadmill that makes you pump just to keep where you are. Gradually it slows, reaches a manageable speed just above normal. I hear bickering, though I can't understand the subject. The boys poke one another drunkenly, their voices getting closer, until it appears they've agreed on something, seemingly related to the flagpole, slapping one another's shoulders. Overhead the moon rides the chop of clouds, blurred like a wet cottonball. I watch it bob across the sky, then turn and see Alexandre take out a pocket knife and open it and hand it to Oscar, who puts the knife between his teeth and starts clumsily up the pole. A few feet up, he loses his hold, stubs his hand on a metal eye, and crashes to the bottom, cursing, grabbing, shaking his hand.

For some reason I pick the knife off the ground and put it between my teeth and start climbing, hugging the pole hard between my knees and feet, shimmying up a foot or two at each pull, thinking that when I get to the top I'll figure what to do, whether to deface the flag, whatever it says, or to cut it down. I reach up, drag myself farther. I'm halfway up, getting closer, head swimming, vertiginous over the swaying lot, the figures of the boys yelling encouragement, when I hear a shotgun blast and its echo. Something whistles way overhead, damn. I freeze and then start down, trying not to burn my hands, dropping the final feet onto my right foot. Ricardo helps me up, his arm around my neck, and I turn in the direction of the shot to see an old man leaning out of a doorway shaking a gun in the air. Alexandre picks up a soda bottle from the littered yard and tosses it so that it explodes a few feet in front of the man. The man swears and the boys swear back, and when something they say really scores he fires another round, the retort closer to our heads. He lowers to reload, fires again, laughing crazily, and we scram in all directions. Ricardo whizzes by on the motorcycle. My ankle stings; I'm trotting down an alley, the old man's curses fainter.

The jeep is parked by a large building made up as a disco. A mirrored ball spins over a dance floor; tables ring the floor; cubes of light swim and glitter against the limitations of a bare, peeling wall. Funk-percussion rocks my jeans. Above the bar a bottle-shaped sign saying LIBIO alternates between pink and blue neon too rapidly.

Half a dozen sad-looking men court every woman in the place. Ricardo and Oscar sit down at our table with an enormous woman who has her arms around them and a beer in one hand and smells like a striped bass. In the center of the floor a grand Teutonic dancer spins, wearing a glittering nose ring, lavender spiderweb-patterned tights, and earrings in both ears—one so long and involved it looks like a Walkman disappearing into a tassled leather jacket—her hair bristling green in front and flowing long and straight blue in back. Five guys spiral with uneven and it seems slow giddiness around her like bugs in a camper headlight. She's not looking at them or paying attention to anything but the physical act of dancing, her own hard rhythms, and yet she seems vaguely aware of them, dancing against them, making thrusts up close to them, head averted, that ignore individual contact, as if they're moving obstacles.

The room turns at a slower and slower gait, bodies moving as if they're straining within a clear liquid glue, until I'm half-dreaming, lifted into those nights when, even after hours of slamming at the restaurant, even using the sink as white noise, sleep in the apartment was out, every sound in the hallway Julie, apologetic in a diaphanous nightgown. And I'd get up, feeling the gnaw and pull of the House of Backgammon, craving tension, the relief even of those nights when you get so reconciled to losing that you want it to happen. I would stuff some cash in my pockets and, barely able to suppress a run, jog through the frost-whitened streets toward speed chess with sucker executives or backgammon chuettes with the Bulgarians, who dubbed me "honorary Bulgarian" and let me drink from their communal snifters. And the nights would pass in sounds, sounds of the dice rattling in the cups and dropping, dancing on the board, and sounds of checkers on worn cork, arranging the prime, almost a tune, the slap of checkers making different notes, checkers kissing the curves of other checkers (chink-chink-chink), checker against cork (thud), the hollower sounds of hit checkers slapped against the wood bar dividing the board, sounding like lots of things, large raindrops, a distant axe.

"Boy," Slav the Bulgarian calls into the darkness of the disco. "Come here, my boy. You want play backgammon?"

He wears a service shirt that says OUR PLEASURE TO SERVE YOU on it and has a spreading pink ink stain below the pocket from sweat on a pen, and he's got on a felt hat with the sort of crushed duck feather that Tom uses to make flies.

"Okay, I'm in?" I ask.

"Sure, sure you in," Figaro the Barber says, his arms askew and moving, his hair combed strangely over an angular sun-blotched skull.


The spangled disco walls turn amazingly and slow, winding down to a stop, until there are just a few couples slow-dancing. Mostly boys with boys, no women in the place anymore, the boys somehow looking slighter and almost fragile, their hands laced around each other's shoulders or waists.

Two boys walk by hand in hand.

Then another couple of boys pass, their fingers interlocked lightly. It hurts to move my head. One boy's face is black and blue, the swelling and smudge a dull rise.

"Bobby," a voice says behind me. "Bobby, what you saying something, Bobby. Bobby, you so very funny sometime."

"Hey," I say, not turning.

"Come, Bobby."

"What?" I say, turning.

"You and I."

"Alexandre," I say.

He stumblewalks to the table, places one forearm on the table. With the other hand he touches my fingers, then runs his hand fully over mine.

"Come, Bobby," he says, a slur in his voice, a glazed, affectionate look in his eyes.

I look into his eyes, feeling a hazy, exhausted sadness, like I'm already out of and away from this somehow scripted night.

"Come, Bobby," he says, voice gentle and, strangely, after his recklessness in the corral—after the flips and shots he's taken, the tenacious gettings up after—now timid. "We go outside, Bobby. You and I. We take walk."

"Not now," I say.

"Why not, Bobby?"

I shake my head slightly, turn my hand slowly in his and squeeze his fingers in a semihandshake, with the other hand doing the French twist of the fist over the nose to say I'm smashed, Jonesed, that it'd be dodgy to attempt movement.

"What you say, Bobby?"

"Not now, Alexandre," I say, and let my head rest again on the table.

"Okay, Bobby. Bobby Washington," he says, his voice seeming already distant, the touch of his hand running over the bristles of my hair seeming light like a breeze.


I wake on a splintery wood floor, first puzzled by how bruised I am, then seeing those steers. Two oblong shapes overhead clear into focus, becoming wood ceiling beams. The shoelace burns and pulses on my left foot. A fetid smell drifts up from the vicinity of my shirt. The boys lie sprawled like a trench-war photo, limbs at improbable angles, faces dirt-smudged but peaceful. I dress and wander, limping slightly, through a high-ceilinged hall, then go outside and piss in the bushes.

Back inside, the owner of the ranch sits at a long wood table drinking steaming milk. He nods to me and motions for me to sit across from him. He sips from the milk and dunks a hunk of black bread into it, then calls to his wife in Portuguese. His wife enters, dressed all in black, and places a pitcher of hot milk and a glass and a hunk of the hard black bread in front of me. I thank her. The owner motions for me to dip the bread in the milk; the warm skim-taste barely softens the bread. We eat in silence. I glance at him several times—he's concentrating on his bread. After we're done, I motion that I need my sack and am ready to hit the road. He rises, we walk out to the jeep and I sling the sack over my shoulder and hold out my free hand, but he shakes his head, points to a backless truck. When we get to the side of the main road south he stops, motions me for a piece of paper. I take out my hitching pad and he writes the name of his ranch on it, and something else. The letters don't seem to spell anything, like an eye test.

"Boa viagem e boa sorte, Roberto Washington," he says.

# 3

There's an ape fetus in the freezer of the Paris loft where Yvonne's living with a Québecois painter named Quinn Beaumont. The place belongs to an ape specialist who's off doing field research in Gabon. The walls of the loft are covered with R. B. Kitaj reprints, framed wildlife posters, close-ups of chimpanzees and baboons, grinning, rubbing their eyes, group shots, and then hundreds of charcoal sketches of Yvonne in various postures, all haphazardly pinned to the walls. I move to get a closer look at one but freeze, feeling watched, then wheel to see a life-size orangutan in the corner, the creature's arms held up as if it's hanging from an absent tree or stomping a jungle jig, but stuffed.

Julie and Yvonne were housemates in college. I met Julie at one of Yvonne's theme parties: the invitation said to bring something with Q in it. I stopped at a bar on the way and borrowed a pool cue. Julie made a horse out of Q-Tips with hoofs of quarters, rider carrying a Q-Tip lance. Junior and Senior breaks, Julie and I went camping in the Smokies with Yvonne and her friend Dave, usually during the off-seasons of mists, cloud-smoke, and tropical green lichens. Yvonne sometimes went with someone else. She and Dave had an arrangement. If they went with someone else they just wouldn't tell.

"Why give medicine before the patient's sick?" I asked.

"That's right," Yvonne said. "Never volunteer information."

This must have been Julie's logic when she started seeing The Hallmark Card. True, people never tell each other everything. They keep a kicker in the hole. And that's fine. Or do you rate something, enough to know whether to fight or fold?

Every day on those trips we each spent a few hours alone. A truly Julie idea. Julie nestled against a tree and read. I fished. Late at night Julie and I, primed by coffee, played Scrabble by candlelight in the tent, Julie staring at her tiles, sizing up all the combinations, a perturbed concentration around her eyes, oddly stern in the shifting shadows. She likes to win at everything—wouldn't think of playing without keeping score—and when she finally spots the killer play she lays her tiles out.

"Now count up, Jason," she says, clasping her hands in front of her, looking delighted and impishly devious in her long johns.

Once, wading upstream, flicking my fly against the bank with a roll cast, I saw Yvonne lying on the bank in a wedge of sunlight with nothing but a tree shadow draped over one leg. The water was low and clear. A slight snow runoff made the water too cold to swim in long, though the air was warm in the sun. No mayflies were hatching, so I used a #14 Royal Coachman that sat high and white even in the bubbles and dazzle-sheen of the water. The fly traced patterns over water so clear you could see uncatchable trout at the end of the pool shooting off in crazy angles. I trained my eyes on the white hairs of the Coachman dancing a riffle, watched it change pace, lazy then stretching out, paying out the slack with my left hand, and was directly across from her when I saw her propping herself slowly on her elbows, looking straight at me, head tilted slightly. I couldn't read the look; part of her game is always to angle for response, seem at once risqué and as unconscious of her effect on others as possible. She made no move to cover herself, but arched her back, as if stretching, breasts momentarily pointing skyward, hair sliding over her shoulders. Though I'd seen her naked several times, skinny-dipping on Fire Island or incompletely blanketed around driftwood fires, this was the first time sober, alone, in daylight. My breath caught, which she saw. There was a stillness and lushness to the landscape.

"Come and sit with me," she called.

My flyline slid over a ripple and then swung wide downstream so the fly dragged and went under. I reeled in, air-dried the fly and stuck it into the cork handhold of Tom's rod, then waded toward the edge of the stream until we were maybe five feet apart, the cold water still locking my ankles. My jeans were soaked to midthigh, and my legs shivered as I stepped out of the water and set the rod down gently against a rock.

"How's fishing?" she asked.

"I've got breakfast," I said.

I slipped the creel over my head and laid it on the grass, then shook off my vest. Yvonne opened the creel and looked at the four small, bright brookies.

"They're nice," she said. "You smell like fish."

"So do you," I said.

She laughed so hard that Julie, off somewhere writing "yesses" in the margins of *Being and Nothingness*, probably dropped her pen.

"There's nothing wrong with looking," Yvonne said, sitting up and shaking ground stuff out of her hair.

"Who said there was?" I said. "There'd be an investigation if I didn't."

She feigned peevishness, fluttered her eyelashes. "You haven't really looked yet. And wouldn't you be just a wee bit interested *if* I were interested?"

"Are you?"

"You know, Jason," she said, "the only reason people don't do exactly what they want is cowardice."

I hesitated, turning the statement over a few ways, then put my hand on her thigh.

"Let's say I'm interested," she said, rolling onto her side. "How about you, Jason?"

"Thanks," I said. "That's awfully nice of you."

"No. Because of Julie, right?" she said.

"You *were* counting on that," I said, too lamely.

She put her hand on mine.

"The day you question this, this . . . let's call it *code*, of yours," she said, "I'll start the investigation."


Yvonne and I have souvlaki with red-pepper sauce in St.-Michel and then start, arm in arm, across the avenue-wide bridge passing Notre Dame.

"You see anyone?" Yvonne asks.

"Few psychotics," I say.

"Like?"

"Like this woman who said she was having a telepathic relationship with a movie star."

"Which star?"

"She wouldn't say."

"Why not?"

"Thought he'd be listening. I told her she shouldn't walk home alone, and she said she wasn't alone. Then she started leaving messages on my answering service that she'd broken up because of me and wanted to kill herself. Then there was a woman who almost bit my arm off. Look."

"Your arm's fine," she says, not really looking at it. "You're as bad as Quinn."

We've been walking in circles through spray-painted lanes

looking for the Bar Fitzcaraldo. Now we step out onto a boulevard and Yvonne asks a waiter at an outdoor café for directions.

"Oui, ça existe," he says.

"Mais où?" I say.

"Je n'sais pas exactement où," he says, with a look of Gallic consternation, twirling his waxed mustache. "Mais ça existe. J'en suis sûr."

"Thanks," I say.

"Pas de question, ça existe," he says, lost in thought.

The bartender at Fitzcaraldo wears suspenders and has hands that look like pet-aids for training Dobermans. His forearms are immense and veined. A soused Slavic woman comes running up and throws her arms around me and crushes a kiss on my cheek that sounds like a suction cup releasing, as if she's been watching Armistice Day reruns.

You ask yourself at some point, staring at a skyline of bottles, the Eiffel Tower Galliano: do I want to get oblivious? You're still marginally sober when you ask this. Or maybe you just think you are. We sip *vin ordinaire*. I'm exhausted from the day's hitch and feel myself drifting into a hazy, purple, private zone from which I can still hear Yvonne and register what she says with nods but from which I am already thinking how nice it would be to slip away and sip alone, and then lie by a fountain or under a bridge, sliding into those wine-logged dreams from which you wake with a mild hangover and large thoughts.

"Still walking out of movies in which people kiss?" Yvonne asks.

"No," I say. "But I think about her, sure."

Yvonne puts her arm around me.

"It happens."

"I'll see someone that looks like her . . ."

"Jason, please. You're giving me a contact low."

"Don't worry, I'm out of that . . . soup," I say.

"And the casinos?"

Yes, I nod. But immediately I wonder if I'm being so recovered because it might get back to Julie. Yvonne's been in Paris five months. They were always into swapping postcards. You never have the same place in people's minds that they have in yours, but I'd like Julie to know I'm okay. In case it matters to her, which it probably doesn't.

"I hate how I acted," I say.

"Sure," she says. "But things change."

"Yeah," I say. "Once there were sturgeon in the Hudson River. There were fox and deer in Central Park."

Back at the loft we drink hot cider spiked with Calvados and then open a bottle of Barbera with Quinn, who has just finished twelve hours of work on a diptych and wears a smock that apparently doubles as an impasto palette. His mood shifts quickly, like his movements. His energy depresses me, both because of my own listlessness and because there's a sadness in it. I find myself watching what seems the thin perpetual charade of those so serious they can't face life without theatrical screens. Problems arise with this when you act so many parts that you don't know which one to believe, or when you sicken of the surfaces presented to you because you don't open up. So be it, I think. The dark red wine has a fine, peppery nose.

"Does my tongue appear green to you?" Quinn asks me, coughing deeply.

"Quinn swears his tongue's green," Yvonne says.

"It does look a bit green," I say.

"Don't encourage his delusions, Jason," Yvonne says. "And Quinn, honey. There's a patch of your face you haven't shaved."

When Quinn's not talking he twirls his wine glass between thumb and forefinger or picks up an ashtray or corkscrew, or stares at a twisted piece of plastic wrapper, studying them like he's examining modern sculpture. There's Montreal Frenchness in his accent. Quinn's tall and gaunt, but his skin and face are almost babyishly smooth, out of keeping with his height, the slope of his cheekbones and his very bushy dark eyebrows. He moves with the awkward springiness of the unathletically angular. He got his M.F.A. from Cranbrook Academy a few years back and has had mixed-media installations in New York and Paris. There are art books and French and Italian exhibit catalogues all over the place. I keep looking askance at the orangutan; when I turn my head he looks like he's moving.

"So where's next?" Yvonne asks, following my glance. "You know, you could hang out here for a few days."

"Where next?" I muse, thinking how in the countries with coded licenses like France the last two digits on the plate often tell you where the car is heading. Otherwise, you can ask the driver where he's going and then answer excitedly that you're going there too, wherever—does it matter?

"Where next is a question," I say.

"Ah, the wanderer," Quinn says, with mock solemnity. "He becomes aimless because he has a terror for tiny dreams."

While we sip, Quinn sketches my head with charcoal on a pad, babbling rapidly at the same time, a constant seriocomic patter meant to distract me from motion while keeping him focused. Not conversation. Like the ironic chatter of dentists who know full well that, your mouth pried open, full of suction, a drill in their hands, they can bait you with any outrageous statement, sure you can't bite. Only my hands move, bringing wine to my mouth.

"There is a global displacement going on, you know," Quinn says. When he speaks, patches of red and white appear on his cheeks and neck, giving his complexion a piebald look. "The Americans occupy Germany so the Germans spread over Europe. In Greece there are villages with no Greeks. When the Moroccans make *un quartier latin* of Paris the Latinos make one of New York."

I glance toward Yvonne, but she's immersed in reading ads in a slick French architecture magazine.

"Everywhere this is happening," Quinn says, waving his emptied wine glass, which, breaking the pose briefly, I take from his hand and fill.

"Merçi beaucoup. Paris is becoming a museum. Soon they will have to charge admission for passes into the city. You will see this. Only tourists or condo owners will sleep here."

"And hitchhikers?"

"Yes, American hitchhikers, looking for something. They have everything so they want to try less, especially in a different language."

When he's done Yvonne tears the sketch out of the pad and pins it alongside her own face and that of a middle-aged baboon. We sit for a few minutes without talking, pour ourselves halfway down a new bottle of Barbera. I ask Quinn about his painting. He starts describing the diptych: on each canvas there is a barely distinguishable face painted with thick oils and added materials, like bits of newspaper and clothes buttons. The two canvases are set at right angles, half facing each other, half looking out. For hair he uses yarn, most of the yarn hanging, but a few yarns connect one head to the other. The connected hairs will look slightly on end, but they will form a pattern, Quinn says, his voice suddenly seeming tired and raspy, his movements slower. Yvonne looks up from the magazine at him. Clearly, they're ready for bed. So I say I've about had it and get my sleeping bag and spread it on the floor.

When Yvonne comes out to see if I'm comfortable enough a few minutes later, I just murmur, though from the moment my head hit the floor I've realized that it's one of those nights when, wired into every sound, tired beyond exhaustion in a forced second wakefulness, I'll never sleep.

In the next room Quinn and Yvonne whisper softly and after a respectful interval start making love, trying, no doubt, to be quiet, whispering, but their muffled noises—exhalations, muted laughs, the faint suck of a mouth on a breast, that squeaky play of springs, the soft scratching of skin over skin and mattress—give me the picture. I lie there, facing the ceiling. There's no point trying not to hear, no way to stop attaching gesture to sound, an odd sense of participation and kind of relief when they are at last still.

Then I get up and stretch a few times. It's got to be late. With the first light I'll hit a pastry shop for a *tarte abricot* and then head out for the road. I tiptoe to the kitchen and pour half a glass of the Barbera, admire its deep glow, then empty the bottle into my glass and move to the window, and stand there, feeling alone. A catalogue of Francis Bacons from a Parisian show rests on the window sill, diptyches and triptyches of twisted figures, muscles exposed, as if flayed; in one, a man retching over a toilet, his back ringed by ovals of yellow light that could as well be reflections of my wine glass on the glossy reproductions. I look at the man for maybe ten minutes, until I realize that at some point I've stopped really looking at him. The night is dark and warm, streets empty, oddly quiet, magnifying the occasional distant laughs of parties breaking up, people stumbling against trash cans, and every now and then a siren.

# 4

It is with hitching as with fishing. There's technique, stance, patience, probabilities, randomness, that delicious uncertainty, the inevitable what-ifs, the process itself. Early starts and the midday lulls and empty days and urgency at sundown. The knowledge that you can't raise anything without having your fly on the water. The last ten cars, then ten more casts, and how many times on the last thumbs-up have you raised a car? Slow times, solitude and spaces, moments of heartsickness in the deeper, cooler stillness, tanned arms, little rides, the connection at the end of the line, the mountable trophy. It is perhaps no coincidence that one speaks of a *stream* of traffic or of *casting* glances at drivers or *catching* a lift or *hooking up* with a car. You hike out, improving your position, moving through something large, until you get to the good place on the bank of the road, maybe a junction pool where streams of traffic join and swirl, forcing slownesses, activity and collision, lucrative zones of slack, and you wade out as far as safety allows. If someone has already claimed your spot, you walk by, exchange a few civil questions whose answers you'll distrust—*how far? how long?*— stop a respectable distance downstream. Then you must attend to presentation, matching your dress to the area, making a sign, finding that right angle. But the best preparations aside, there just might not be any cars going your way. And if there are, and the pool's jumping, dappled by fish kissing the surface, one unending procession of headlights stippling the dawn, who's to say how they'll be biting?

I camp outside Pompeii next to three Swedes who smoke hash and play the guitar all day, rarely leaving the campsite. Mornings they invite me for coffee. One day I hike off trail up the hardened splashes of lava where surges cooled on Vesuvius, picture that twenty-three-foot layer of ash settling over Europe, those ribby, wide-socketed people, legs bent against the on-surge, hands fending off the unfendable. None of them would have lasted, I think, without the lava. Another day I walk around the ruined city below, find a stump of column on the via dell'Abbondanza to read on. Bright red poppies bloom all around, a small gray green lizard bites a leaf, head darting, stomach pounding. It licks its lips and vanishes against rocky fragments. A British couple emerges from the ruins of someone's bed chamber with a pleased, guilty look, and waves. I stare at the surrealistic edges of doorways silhouetting nothing, sometimes with people's initials scratched into them, thinking: Maybe these carvings will be tomorrow's runes, and spray-paintings in subway tunnels will be discovered like the Altamira caves. After a week I get that itch to cover ground.

The first night I end up in the train station in Rome next to an old man in a three-piece suit who keeps a ticket for Florence in his pocket. He tells me in a heavily accented English that the *polizi* make a ticket check once in a while but tonight they might not because it's so cold. He has family in New Jersey and some-a-day, some-a-day he will visit them. He begs me to see St. Peter's Basilica the next day, telling me in a tired but excited voice about the magnificence and sacredness of the place.

"The Romans, what power they had, they could afford it," he says. "They had-a the gold, they conquered all-a the world."

I tell him that in the morning we'll find a café and eat hot rolls with jelly together and then he can show me the Vatican jewels and the Chapel. Then I tell him to get some sleep and I'll wake him if the *polizi* come.

Somehow, no matter what station you're waiting in late at night, you feel like you've been there before, every face saying, *Sir, you look poor, but I'm poorer. Let me hold a few.* Maybe those other times were dress rehearsals for the time you'd really cut out. The night Julie and me fought, I was in the bus station at Atlantis and some blind man with a scrofulous seeing-eye dog was bumping and pawing his way around the perimeter of the room. A half-gone loaf of Wonder Bread hung from the man's belt. Derelicts and head cases hooted him until he got to the soda machine and started roving his hands over the raised plastic buttons.

"What kind of soda you want?" I asked.

"May you have God's speed," he said. "Reach me an Orange Crush."

There's a man curled on the floor without shirt or shoes and a gaunt woman circling entries in an old TV section. I hand them both tangerines I picked up at a roadside fruit stand. I had tried to explain to the guy at the fruit stand that I wanted to pay, but he kept babbling at me, making me drink from a wine skin, the words *friend* and *journey* and *more* much repeated. I kept stuffing the tangerines he handed me into my sack, and forgot them until now. They're bright and full of juice. When another bum sees me distributing tangerines he moseys by.


"You don't have to go home, but you can't stay here," Fred always yells at last call.

Around 4:00 A.M. the *polizi* tell all of us who don't have tickets to hit the road. I shake with the old man and walk out toward the autostrada, checking behind to see if I'm being followed. Out on the road, cars whang by. It will be several hours until sunrise; I put on my wool sweater and walk briskly to keep warm. Under a lamplight there's a squashed creature with a thin crimson strip running from its mouth like a tongue that's licked cherry Italian ice.

About an hour down the road I pass a rest area where truck drivers sleep a few hours. There are three trucks. The light goes on in the cabin of one, then blinks off. I pull myself onto the truck step and look in, but the driver's fast asleep. In the next truck a driver's crouching with his pants down over a flabby dark-haired girl whose white breasts spill out from an open shirt. The man hears me, slams his hand against the window, starts cursing; hoarse yells follow me down the road. . . . *Va fan cullo . . . che cazza fai. . . . Stonzo!*

Rose light tints the crests of hills on either side before light hits the road, for an instant drenching it with fluid colors. In the softer morning light, braced against a cold wind, the road stretches flat and bare for as far as I can see. I stand with my sketch-pad held out and then walk at a steady gait, pressing up with a kind of pleasure against the empty, tired feeling, half hoping I'll lose track of my feet and just walk for hours. Time slides by; the sunlight hardens, still cold and crisp. Then a car stops abruptly up ahead of me.

"Luigi," the driver says. "And what is your name?"

"Jason," I say.

"Jacob?"

He pantomimes a man climbing. I shake my head.

"Jason non e importanta," he says. "Jacob importanta. Come diciamo in italiano, Jacob is for me mucha more importanta."

He's got a small round face, black hair, and exhausted blue eyes. He's wearing a black sports jacket over a white silk shirt split to show pale rolls of stomach. A plastic Madonna decked with beads beckons from the dashboard. I rub my hands together, blow into them, massage each finger.

"Is warmer in here, no?" Luigi says, glancing at me with raised eyebrows. "Is okay we practice my English a little?"

He looks at me and smiles, drumming his fingers nervously along the steering wheel.

"I like to take up hitchhikers," he says.

An orange rolls back and forth across the floor over what looks like a Christian Boy Scout fashion magazine. My lips are crusted and chapped.

"From what city are you?" Luigi asks, fingers still playing along the wheel.

"New York."

He shifts in his seat and steps on the gas, jolting the car forward, stroking his belly. Then he gives a high, teapot whistle through his teeth and looks at me again. It is warmer in the car and I lean back, feeling the road hard, unending, slip-sliding away, perpetually seeming to narrow but never getting any narrower, always staying between the same onrushing boundaries, the road a train track, and Luigi's whistle now an engineer's.

"You make a vacation?"

"Take a vacation. Yes."

"You like New York. Is very large, no? Very big city."

Luigi laughs, the sound emerging from his white belly, his lips barely moving. A humorous, wild light enters his eyes, like he's recalling some sick joke funny only to him. I pick up the orange, and Luigi nods and gives the low whistle through his teeth. I concentrate on peeling the orange and not looking at him. I'd like to glue his tapping fingers to the wheel. When I'm done with the orange I close my eyes as if I'm tired and need rest, and try to drift from the scene, thinking of a Paris breakfast of a glazed *tarte fraise* with custard and an almond croissant, of the way the bread flakes off and the custard filling at the center saturates the thin surrounding leaves, of how you peel the layers away and use your finger on the custard as on a dip.

Very softly Luigi puts his hand on my thigh. I don't realize it at first but when I do I just take the hand and place it on the seat beside me. Neither of us speaks. Luigi's face looks serious, lips pressed together. He sits straight, eyes trained straight out at the road, the knuckles of one hand white on the steering wheel.

On a long drive through Connecticut to visit Julie at her folks' summer house, a traveling salesman tried to talk me into jacking off in the front seat.

What a weekend.

Such savage cordiality. Julie's parents acted like they'd stepped out of *Better Homes and Gardens*. Her father, edgily amused by my hitching, peeled off his gardening gloves to shake, then led us into a glass-covered conservatory. There we sat in wicker chairs and were refreshed by iced tea.

He's actually calling me into his study for a man-to-man, I thought later, as I followed Julie's father after dinner. Next he's going to ask after my plans. *Plans, sir?* I could ask, dumbfounded. But maybe if I make a good impression he'll offer cash to buy a treat for his little princess. Later, in fact, he did assist us with Julie's half of the rent, a perk, since Julie is one of those people on parental welfare who works low-paying jobs, keeps an index file of Oodles of Noodles recipes (someday she'll write the Oodles of Noodles cookbook), and has a charge account at Saks.

"So what are your plans?" he asks the second I sit across from him at his mahogany desk. Case studies spread neatly before us; a wooden decoy and ceramic Brittany spaniels grace the desk.

I consider, *Human Resource Management, sir. Fast foods.* Or,

*Sir, what matter so long as I, like your delectable daughter, add more joy to the world than I take out?*

"Well," I say. "I'm weighing several options."

He looks like he wants to say something else, something warmer, but can't think of a way to do so.

"I'll be taking the LSAT's and the GRE's this fall."

"I'm sure you'll do very well," he says, laughing uneasily. "Julie says you're . . . quite the student."

"She said that, sir? Really?"

"Yes, Jason. Call me Reginald, okay?" he says, nodding.

"Yes, sir, I mean, Reginald."

That night Julie slipped into my room. That slender gold cross of hers skate-hopped like a waterbug over my chest. I could hear it whispering over our breath in that house, *Any, oh god, good Catholic's basically anti-Catholic.* She made so much noise laughing, moaning, and wrestling she must have meant them to hear. At first she was biting my neck in a way so unnecessarily hard it could hardly be considered an attack of passion, and I thought she was pissed over some faux pas—a nose-pick at the table, some sense of my not being presentable—though clearly she enjoyed rubbing her parents in that. At any moment I expected Reginald to bust through the door, backed by servants carrying hedge clippers and andirons. I woke in my four-poster bed, weak light passing through ridiculous nursery pink-lace canopies, illuminating botanical wallpaper, my neck throbbing, and my body weak from one of those dreams where in a crowded room a posse of tuxedoed people takes turns slapping you around.

At breakfast Reggie kept shooting glances at my hickey. I'd turned my collar up to hide most of the damage. I battled an impulse to ask Julie whether the hand-painted plates were dry. She kept squinting at me. Anyone's impeccable behavior or good posture has always seemed to me coldly insane. Julie's mother might have been a centerfold for *Better Homes and Gardens*. Mrs. Jejeune. Hair flawless. It's at most 9:00 A.M. and she's wearing a red riding vest patterned with assorted ducks and a gold bugle-shaped pin. She eats with a rectitude suggesting anality, chewing with a faint smile liable to switch from grin to withering severity without transition, like a game show contestant's.

"Relax," the traveling salesman had said. "Take off your shoes, but if your feet stink, leave them on."

We were sliding through a sequence of churches, restaurants, warehouses that all looked like bowling alleys.

"How'd you like to make a quick fifty bucks?" he asked.

"Thanks, but no," I said.

"You know what I mean?"

"I think I know what you mean."

"Really?"

"Yeah, I think so."

"Well. What do you think I mean?"

"Okay, you tell me what you mean."

He says he'll just pull the car off by the side of the road and keep his hands to himself. Be the easiest money you ever made, he says. Get paid for something a healthy boy like you must do twice a day anyway, minimum. Nothing to it.

"How about a hundred?" he asks.

I tell him it isn't a question of money and that I'm on my way to see my *girlfriend*.

"You're a hard salesman," I say, immediately regretting my diction. "But you've got to know when you're not going to close a deal, okay?"

He laughs at that and, to change the subject, I ask him about sales. "To put it in lay terms," he begins, and proceeds to talk about hard-sell tactics, budget implementation, cash flow problems, liquidity planning until I swear that if I hear one more double entendre I'm going to jump out of the car. But ten minutes later he asks me why I won't do it. A fair enough question. Why not? It's a roll on the dice, a possible sequence. Why not just whip it out and take the man's cash? But you never know what will happen when you bare your parts. We're vulnerable enough without exposing ourselves.

When I tell some of the guys in the House of Backgammon about it they tell me I'm crazy.

"I'd have done it for twenty as many times as he wanted," Piano says. "And it would have cost him."

Piano uses his palm as an ashtray, then sprinkles the ashes over the floor and wipes his hands on his pants.

"You'd do it for five *if* you could do it once," Acer says, stripping a ten from a roll in his baggy pants and slapping it on the table. "But I'll pay you ten. Go ahead right now."

"Go ahead, Piano, here's ten more," Chemicals says.

Figaro's making passes over the remaining hairs on a deaf old man's head, flourishing a long pair of scissors.

"I'd never drop trou around you guys," Piano says, shaking his head. "Never. Look at Figaro with those scissors."

"Figgy'll give you a special cut, all right," Acer says.

"Don't get Figgy excited," Chemicals says.

"What did you say?" the deaf old man asks.


The feel of Luigi's hand shocks me out of my thoughts. I feel his hand on my thigh again, starting to massage upward, as if he's started soft and maybe I didn't feel it at first. Luigi looks straight ahead at the road. The hills slide by; beads rattle on the Madonna.

"Luigi," I say, trying to arrange a reasonable tone.

But he doesn't answer, just whistles. The hand, seemingly acting on its own impulses, inches up, massaging my thigh a centimeter at a time, a firmness in his fingers.

"Luigi," I yell, wrenching his hand from my thigh. He lets go without resistance, his eyes altering only slightly at the bite of my nails on his wrist; he purses his lips. It strikes me I've yelled and that it's strange to have yelled the name of someone I don't know in the car, just the two of us.

"No thanks, okay, Luigi," I say. "Capisco?"

"Oh, I am so very very sorry," he says. "So sorry. On the honor of my mother, I understand."

"Good," I say.

We drive, speed steadily increasing, until we're moving too fast, unevenly along the road. Luigi pulls himself up and makes sudden surges, gripping the wheel tightly with both hands, a manic amusement in his eyes. The odometer passes two hundred kilometers, the car rattling increasingly. Framed by the windshield, the road rushes up at me like a movie screen during a chase.

"Luigi," I say, quickly.

Nothing. No response.

"Hey, Luigi."

I close my eyes. Speed invades my muscles, tears at them. Faster still, until there's only sheer speed, the car about to bend or fishtail against laws of inertia. And then a sharp agonizing thrill leaps through my body to the highest hairs on my head and crashes back into my genitals where Luigi's hand has grabbed them.

"No!" I yell, grabbing his hand with all my strength, and mashing it against the dashboard.

"Stonza," he yells, hands leaving the steering wheel, one hand grabbing the banged one in the air. The car seems to spring out of control, heading for the side of an underpass. There's a furious look on his face, like he's about to explode. I unfasten my seat belt and lunge for the wheel but he beats me to it, pushes my hand away, and then we're driving very slowly, and slower still, and pull to the side of the road.

"You get out," Luigi screams, still rubbing his hand, making occasional hurt noises, almost whimpers, and flicking the hand in my direction.

I open the front door and the back door.

"Get out, American boy," he yells at the side of my face, spit hitting my cheeks, my ears ringing.

I wipe his spit on the dashboard, shove my sack out of the back onto the road, and then leap out, slamming both doors. I kick-slide my sack into the grass and squat, then lie down on my side. My nuts throb sharply from being ground against each other. The grass is soft and the sun shines brightly. I roll over in the grass, still slightly curled. There are no clouds; the sky is a pastel blue.

After a minute I sit up and rummage in my sack for a map. The pain between my legs has become a steady pulsing, the moment of shock replaying itself in miniature with each welling, my heart still beating hard through images of my hand crunching his knuckles against the dashboard and of the car exploding in double balls of flame against the underpass, my pulse going the way it does when you slalom through a string of ill-advised double-or-nothing bets, any of which will wipe you out. There are a few tangerines left and a slightly hard end of bread. I chew the bread slowly and then peel the tangerines and split them carefully into sections and edge off the strands of pith. I lay the tangerine sections out on the map. It's only about eighty miles to Verona, I estimate, and I'm on a roll, feeling strong, that momentarily cheering sense that you'll be able to deal with mistakes you haven't yet made. I can walk all day, read if I want, walk through the night. I bite into a section and chew it slowly, trying to wet every part of my mouth.

# 5

I'm sitting by the road reading a mystery called *The Trojan Horse*
I traded for in a youth hostel; I've walked for a few hours. Now
my hitching pad is propped on my sack saying VERONA. In the
book a spy has just sent his eighty-seven-year-old grandmother
behind the Iron Curtain with microfilm surgically implanted in
her buttocks. An expendable character's just been killed, sloppily, when a red Alfa Romeo speeds by. The car drives slowly
for a stretch, and then backs toward me, growing larger until it
stops only a few feet away. A woman leans, then hops out,
smiles cheerfully, opens the trunk, motions for me to toss my
sack in. She moves with a slightly exaggerated rotation at one
knee that she doesn't seem to notice.

"Grazie," I say. "It was a long walk."

"I no speaking English," she says. "Io sono Rosalie."

"Io Jason," I say. "Italiano, non capisco."

"Ohhhhhhh," she sighs, "Madonna. Is okay, yes?" Rosalie
shrugs her auburn hair over her shoulders.

"Vous parlez français?" I ask. "Oder Deutsch?"

"Non," she laughs. "Solamente Italiano."

I nod and lay back. My shins ache from the walking.

"Italia," Rosalie says, and puts her thumb up, then shakes so-so, then gives the thumbs-down sign.

I show her thumbs up and say, "Bella, bella."

She looks at me with wide eyes. She has high full cheekbones, and lips that slant upward; her hair's lighter and curlier than Julie's but those eyes are nearly the same size and shade of blue-green as Julie's.

I lie back exhausted and start remembering episodes with Julie, a thing infrequently triggered now, and which I try to choke with memories of times when I wanted to bind and gag her—though Julie might have found that arousing. Early on she asked me to give her commands in bed.

"Close your eyes and don't move," I say in the tent, and start rolling her panties as slowly as I can, stricken almost to the point of breathless wonder as I gather most adolescents are at the incredible fineness and scantiness of panties. I roll them like a master chef rolling leaflike pastry crêpes, hang them on the tent pole, start roving my hands along the insides of her thighs. Julie shimmies to give me the good angle, then freezes.

"What was that?"

We stare out the cheesecloth window, listening, but don't hear anything besides sporadic raindrops snapping against the tent. Mists hover between the trees.

"Lie down now, Fruit Slice," I say. "But have a dog biscuit ready just in case."

"Why is it that every sound makes me think of bears?"

"That poor bear out there is probably more scared of you than you are of him," I say.

"No, he isn't."

Her back scratches slightly against the sleeping bag; the first small involuntary breaths escape.

"Did you clean your fingernails?" she whispers.

"Keep quiet."

I don't like those scenes. But you know how it is. Try not

thinking about pink flamingos and the whole world's the Ever-
glades, Sarasota Downs, or decorations implanted in Long Island lawns.


Rosalie's shaking wakes me. It takes me a minute to realize I'm
not in a drippy tent in the Smokies.

"Verona," she says, laughing, spreading her hands.

I shake my head, slap both of my cheeks.

"Ci," I say.

We sit there for a moment, then I open the door and step out
onto the street. I stretch a few times, gesture for my sack. But
she doesn't move, throws one arm over the empty seat, starts
laughing. I laugh with her a little awkwardly. She holds her head
to one side a little and looks at me, then pantomimes, tucking a
napkin around her neck, a fork entering a mouth, and, humming
*mmmmmmmmmmm*, a well-contented eater rubbing her stomach. Then she says words in Italian and beckons me affection-
ately to get back in the car as you do when you want someone
stupidly obstinate to let go of an argument.

The old buildings, orange and shadow-drenched in the fading
light, have large windows and red-tiled roofs. Stands with bas-
kets of apples and sacks of almonds, shelled walnuts, and pea-
nuts line the streets beneath fringed yellow umbrellas, and little
storefronts have canopies that slant sharply. I motion to one and
say *acqua*, and when she stops I jump out and get us both Coca-
Colas. We sit by a sculptured fountain and a building with or-
nate facades. I guzzle two Cokes, then splash my face with fountain water.

We park outside a small stone building with a high arched
doorway and walk up a narrow spiral of stairs. Her apartment
consists of a long room, a kitchen, mostly wood, flower boxes in
the windows with blooming petunias and pansies. Light filters
through several large stained-glass windows, arranged in vari-

ous patterns: a cluster of multicolored grapes, shells and starfish. There are posters on the walls: Botticelli's Venus on the half shell, an Avercamp silver-skating scene, an Escher, a Modigliani, a slumping Degas absinthe drunk. A thick, braided, patterned rug stretches the length of the room. There's a desk covered with papers against one wall, and Swedish ivy hanging from a shoulder-high bookshelf.

She takes off her sweater, back to me, and slips on a T-shirt, then uses a clothes brush to get sweater hairs from her skirt. I sink into a wicker seat with soft red cushions while she goes into the kitchen and starts boiling water. One could sit in such a wicker seat for a while. But after a few minutes I join her at peeling carrots and cucumbers, and slicing a plate of cheeses.

"Vino?" she asks, holding a bottle of red in one hand, white in the other.

"Bianco."

"Ci. Bianco. Tu parli l'italiano di vini molto bene."

I surmise, "Ci, Bianco, Soave Bolla, Asti Spumante, Follonaro, Chianti Classico, Lambrusco, Rosso Thunderbird."

"Che cosa é rosso Thunderbird?" she says, handing me a wine.

I swirl the glass in front of my nose, a nice aroma, and sample the bouquet. But when my sleeve passes my nose with the wine glass it occurs to me just how much I stink from having slept on several benches and from the train station. When she catches me recoiling from my own stench on a second pass she points to the bathroom, gesturing shower; then she brings several towels and shuts the door behind me. I can't resist a bath and run the hot water. With the first dip you yank your foot back, feeling an echo of heat. I let in a manageable amount of cold water. Right now I could be hiking out along the autostrada in the dark, I think, massaging my shins with a hot washcloth, only I'm here. The heads of the faucets resemble a satyr and a naiad. I shoot the wine, an immediate buzz rising, water steamy and sweat pouring so that I lie back, stewing in my own juices, the road accelerating out behind me.

The smell of garlic, onions, tomatoes, and basil sautéeing in olive oil pervades the room. Rosalie sets a huge bowl of angel hair pasta in front of me, grinds fresh pepper over it. At first I protest that I'm not so hungry, that I couldn't possibly eat that much, just a taste, but before I know it one bowl's gone and then I'm bread-swabbing my reflection a second time in the bottom of the bowl. Rosalie's lips curl upward in amusement. I can't think what to say; all I can do is gesture, rub my stomach, mangle cognates.

We bus the dishes into the kitchen; she washes them and hands them to me to dry, and then she indicates she's going to take a shower. I click on the TV. When she comes out she's wearing a dark robe and towel-drying her hair. We watch a samurai soap opera, Spaghetti Eastern. I sit beside her on the couch, my arm over her shoulder, then turn her slightly, and begin to massage the back of her neck. Her robe shifts, exposing what looks like a burn scar over her knee. I lift the lamp shade to throw light on the scar. Rosalie shields her eyes, watches my face as I trace the edges of the scar, a ridged coastline, like a rash extending from below her knee to midthigh. She lowers her hand and our eyes meet. My hand still grazes the scar. After a minute she closes the robe, brushes my hand away, readjusts the lamp. We finish the table white and open a bottle of red. The samurai takes on a drug ring, his sword mightier than the bullets he repeatedly dodges. But the show is basically a love story, set against delicate budding cherry trees and lush hills, in which the samurai and his loyal, love-smitten geisha address each other in Italian that exits their mouths a second after their lips have stopped moving.

Around midnight I gesture that I can hardly keep my eyes

open after the ample food, the road, the wine. I motion to the couch and shake out my sleeping bag. Rosalie hesitates a moment, then shrugs, and gets a pillow. When she returns I've undressed and slipped into my bag, which smells ripe now that I'm in a house. She stands over the couch for a minute, touches her index finger to my face.

"Buona noté, Jason," she says.

"Grazie, Rosalie. Buona noté," I say.

I drowse right off for what seems like a minute, and then I hear my name whispered as if it's not the first whisper and I've been hearing it and avoiding the call, and I turn and see a figure, a woman, her face dark, faint lamplight at her back, standing spookily a few feet from the couch, her shadow huge, grotesque on the floor. I freeze, not sure where I am or who the woman is or what she wants. If I could move, turn or lift my head, I could see whether she has something in her hand. But I can't move, and feel a strange, terrified stuckness, head ringing with alarm, and the knowledge that I'll only be safe from whatever danger there is when I can move.

"Jason," Rosalie whispers.

With a struggle I spring up, straighten on the couch, heart working crazily. Outlines of the room form, the multicolored windows. I bend, both hands over my face, elbows on my thighs, breathing hard, then sit up again.

"Jason," she says, voice fuller now.

I rub my eyes, in the sudden relief of the room recalling where I am, how I got there. Rosalie is standing, her hand on my shoulder, her touch haunting but light. Her wavy auburn hair falls over the shoulders of a dark robe that glints with silk catchings of lamplight from over by her bed. Her figure gets clearer. For the first time in months I feel hunger and thrill for an unknown body. I haven't slept with anyone since that nerve-numbing interior decorator. Once bitten, twice shy?

"Veni," she whispers, looking at me quizzically.

My legs straighten, as on their own, and I'm standing next to Rosalie, putting my hands on her shoulders. She puts her hands on my stomach. Her hands feel cool. Our lips brush, dusting each other's. She laughs a laugh I don't understand. I'd like to understand but it's not a time to understand anything. I follow to her bed and she parts her robe and slips out of it and stands with her hands in front of her for a moment. Then she laughs again, shakes her hair over her shoulder, climbs into the bed. I step out of my underwear and follow, and when she holds the sheet and quilt off I slide next to her, shivering from the coolness of the sheets.

She cuts off the lamp. Light from outside bends elongated grape shapes across the bed. My eyes adjust again to the dimness. I pull back the sheet and look at our bodies next to each other, white-gray and tinted with colors. I find her hand and press it to my lips and then run my hands lightly over her breasts, which are much fuller than Julie's hard, childlike breasts. Her nipple stiffens; she shudders, shifts my finger away. She kisses my forehead lightly, then kisses lightly and quickly down my nose, like she's going down on my face, and then we kiss fully, and she's sliding over me like a warm wave, and my hand slips over the side of her leg, about the knee, feeling the raised rubberiness of the extended scar, lingering there briefly and then moving upward onto her smooth thigh, my hand continuing up and around, now behind her, following the dampness up her hamstrings.

We kiss and roll, lips ranging, nibbling. Her knees squeeze my hips and gyrate, and when I enter everything momentarily disappears into the slow letting-go roll. But almost as soon as the sensation edges passion, some zone of connection, immersion, release, I'm aware that I've stopped kissing under her arms and along her neck and behind her ears and that she's slowed her movements, as if waiting, as if aware that I've gone out of rhythm, and am elsewhere though still going through motions, though her breath's still warming, wetting my face.

And what comes to consciousness is that Rosalie isn't there anymore, hasn't been. I've whispered or have been whispering *Julie*. And the whisper has gotten louder, become a chorus of whispers slicing each other apart—*Jul-lee*—*leejul*—a round growing to a disruptive decibel. And whether the whisper that started the growing sound was my audible whisper escaping or just my sense of a voice whispering from a seat in the shadowed corner of the room and not my actual whisper doesn't matter. My ears ring with the sound, *Julie, leju, Jul-lee*. Rosalie doesn't seem to hear it. Her legs straddle me, and she's resuming, grinding harder, oddly forceful, pulling me in, drawing me deeper. And as we move, my body involuntarily pressing back against her force, the whisper plays, echoes *Julie* through the room.

CALABACILLAS
THE FOOL

**6**

For two weeks I walk and hitch back roads. On warmer days, feeling like an ant on a giant map, I hike a few hours without my thumb out, stopping in small towns for sandwiches and beer, and then walking out again until it's dark, the asphalt starting to come up through my shoes. At night I lie exhausted, just the road running along in my head, lines on a map: Austria, Germany, curling west through France and then south to the Riviera.

The cool marble hallways of the casino at Nice magnify every sound. People stare at my road dirtiness. I hardly see them; the tables draw me. An hour or so, a hundred bucks ventured, and who knows what gained? I walk with a heightened awareness of the tables in my blood, almost a homing blip in my head that speeds up as I approach, the casino blips merging in a hum.

"Monsieur," a tuxedoed man tells me, gesturing disdainfully at my face and clothes. "You cannot enter the salle like that. Ce n'est pas possible."

The Mediterranean is cold; I swim out a ways, thinking I can cleanse myself and take a crack at the tables, seeing visions of myself turning over cards, scratching the table for a hit, stacking my chips, starting a streak and parlay. But when I'm drying off on the beach I look at the casino and fish for reasons for not going. My hesitation itself, that's one reason. The prospect of showering, shaving, getting fresh clothes—that's another. You want to arrive at a casino and walk straight in and lay the stake on the line, no limits, dust on your clothes or not. Small waves lap my feet. Power consists in being able to say no, I think. Not gambling is also a streak, and I've got one going. I reward myself for not gambling with a two-hour restaurant meal, beginning with a soup called *Soup*, passing through *moules*, ending with *fraise*.

For three weeks I work at a tomato farm outside Evora, Portugal, home of the Chapel of Bones. Above the chapel the sign reads, "Nos ossos que aqui estamos pelos vossos esperamos." *We bones who are here await yours.* The farming pays food and a nominal wage. I work alongside a deaf man, the arcs of our hoes synchronized as we whack away at the hard ground. It is now fully spring, hot and dusty in the fields. Besides the deaf man and me are Serge, a Dutchman; and Jack, destined for the back of a Wheaties box, from French Lick, Indiana, by way of the University of Michigan. Serge pops more vitamins than my stepfather Tom and has walked all the way from Holland. After work he shaves calluses from his feet with an Exacto razor like a kid carelessly carving balsa wood. Serge tells us about how families in Senegal throw their babies under jeep wheels so they can blackmail the drivers. He plans to walk to Algeria to see the blue people, an unspoiled nomadic tribe of flexible dancers and eloquent singers who go blue in the desert heat when indigo from their turbans stains their skin. Plotting the African segment of his trip around the Mediterranean, Jack says he doesn't believe in the blue people because they aren't in his *Let's Go: North Africa*.

"Probably a bunch of grifters who paint themselves with Easter egg dye number two and take American Express," he says, winking knowingly at me.

After three weeks of hoeing and weeding I hitch south, spending the night in a gutted shack with a twenty-year-old Irishman picked up by the same driver. He's fruit-picked through the Loire, headed vaguely for Morocco. The van is filled with neatly stacked vendor cakes. Twenty kilometers down the road the driver lights up a hash pipe. The Irishman and I pass. After a few hits the driver starts giggling, weaving, and then turns suddenly onto a small dirt side road. The Irishman grabs the wheel and the van jumps into a ditch, then halts, dirt thrown onto the window. I work my way out, sling my sack over one shoulder, shovel as many of the cakes as I can into the belly of my half-zipped jacket, and kick-slam the door. The driver's high sweet laugh rolls after us into the absolute dark.

We find the shack after two hours of walking, clear away some of the dust and cobwebs, and rip slats of dry wood off the walls for a fire. He's wearing sandals and carrying nothing but a Mexican blanket and a leather shoulder bag. Maybe one change of clothes and a couple of nesting tins. When the fire's going we split the cream-filled cakes and peel some oranges. Portuguese Twinkies make a fine late snack. Stars beam through the roof; the orange peels curl and pop with a tart, sweet smell. When the cold comes the Irishman wraps himself in his blanket and starts in about factions in Northern Ireland murdering each other. Once he saw a kid impaled on a pitchfork, tines right through his thin, wriggling frame.

When I arrive at the youth hostel in Sagres, Portugal, it is late, just a few people about. I shower and the next morning rise early. The dining room is empty; breakfast won't start for an hour. On a long wood table, half a dozen board games: a German

Monopoly set, Risk, Cribbage. There are pamphlets picturing youths clothed in britches seemingly designed by the von Trapp Family Tailors. Through the window, there's a large stone compass from the old maritime school, laid out and divided up like a sun dial without a stylus. A plaque on the hostel wall no doubt explains how on this site young Bartolomeu and Vasco first prodded makeshift toy sailboats and gazed hopefully at the horizon.

I rummage among the games, turn up a sack of plastic chess pieces and a folded board, start playing blitz against myself. Three minutes total. No aimless, reductive sacking. But repeated temporary plots, contingencies, counterinsurgencies. You shuttle between faith in the attacker and the defense, simultaneously holding and rejecting the black and white viewpoints, the alternating illusions of control, until the positions collapse in sequences of self-betraying, auto-mating combinations. The same hand snuffs and resets. Back to square one, the perfectly balanced drawing board.

I reset the pieces slowly. I haven't seen a set in three months now, since the apartment sale where I peddled, among other worldly goods, one chili Crockpot, one futon, one refinished dresser, a silver-and-obsidian margarita salter from Mexico, an ample stock of Stoli and accompanying silver ice bucket, our high-fidelity stereo, one chandelier bought from a traveling thief-salesman, purveyor of hot deals in the House of Backgammon. We hung it where it cast spinning prismatic sapphires on the dinner table that doubled as a TV stand.


That week before leaving the city, I was just slaughtering executives at chess, beefing my travel roll, stationed in front of my chessboard like a hooker on the highway to Lisbon. The farmers drive by slowly until they see what they want and then go off in the woods. I fleeced a TV programmer in the parlor on Fourteenth Street. His hand trembled on every move, as if he were verging on a seizure. Like most wealthy people who, regardless of talent, come to game rooms knowing they will end up donating pocket money to lowlife, since the regulars play all day and only pick lock games, he was into heavy verbal abuse. Made hopeless cracks after every move. In chess houses you can lose the game but win the commentary, which is okay if you're rich. Though it's hard to say which game a fish prefers losing. I said, *fork you, schmuck*, clapped him in a Shanghai check, and bagged a knight. His face twitched. Then I said *checkalato schmuck* and checked him again, chasing his king out of the pocket, and he didn't get the picture, and I yelled *checkalato again, you schmuck* and he began to see it, and *checkalato once again you absolute schmuckalato* and *yes, okay, calm down*, he said, *yes, yes, don't get excited now, easy, you potzer*, his face stretched out hideously now, contorted, *yes* in the moment of recognition that he could not win but had to go on playing until he was broke, *yes* looking at the shadows of saving moves and knowing them shadows, *yes, okay, calm down, you're a good potzer, yes potzer, calm down potzer, very good, yes.*

Afterward I went out and bought a bagful of honeydews and cantaloupe for the guys and sat with Sammy the Games Philosopher, an old Yiddish chess player, and Yakov, who plays chess for five days and has to be carted to the hospital. An unkempt genius émigré, two rings on every finger, dozens of plastic necklaces, half nut-case, who sleeps on park benches during the day, Yakov can't manage money but is so talented that he can't stay broke and disintegrate with the homeless. The old Yid sleeps by an end game with his mouth open. Yakov dozes in and out, giggling and marveling over a Superwoman comic for adults. Sammy watches as I start playing out the ending.

"Put F6 back," he says, grabbing my hand with surprising

vigor when I lift a wrong pawn. "Put it back, put it back. You play that move and the whole game comes apart."

"I'm getting out of Dodge," I say aloud, thinking, if you can't find anchorage go to Alaska.

"Yeah, I know what you mean," Sammy says, lifting a different pawn. "There, you see. Much stronger. Say, where you headed, kid?"

Sammy went to the nationals in checkers and walks around marking a book called *The Theory and Practice of Backgammon*. On the inside cover of the book Sammy wrote: "Timing equals freedom or greater chances for movement."

A neon light blinks to a brighter consistency with a hum.

"Sun's coming up," Sammy says.

"Don't know where I'm headed," I say. "Maybe Turkey."

"Why?" Yakov says, lifting his head.

"You look like a turkey, Yakov," Pincus the Houseman says, dusting Yakov's back with a hand broom.

"They got backgammon in Turkey?" Sammy asks.

"Don't know, Sammy."

"Then why go there?" Sammy says.


Through the hostel window I see a kid juggling a soccer ball. I watch him alternate the ball from thigh to thigh, and then I turn back to the board and adjust the pieces carefully, seeing lines of play in my head, plotting attack and defense. At first I slide the pieces out slowly, stationing them; then I move with increasing rapidity. The hard opening lines are razor graceful, surgically clean. White lashes out viciously and black lies back, fends and counters; the standard midgame massacre and confusion clears into end game, a passed pawn, rack treatment. Then when it's all inevitable I look up and see that a girl has been watching, maybe even following. I've been vaguely aware of her head following the game with slight, repeated shifts, as if miming a tennis fan's, an amused look on her face, forehead furrowed. I turn away and then look again.

"Who's winning?" she asks, finally.

"It's about even," I say, setting pawns on the table.

There's a delicate fineness to her features; her eyebrows seem too thin, too precise and mobile, as if shaved and then penned in with a Rapidograph. She is excessively freckled, tiny dots that almost blotch around the arms, but evenly tanned, with just a slight pinkness at the end of her nose. She fastens her shock of red, frizzy hair behind her head with an elastic band, a few curls escaping in front. She wears one of those small quartz crystals wrapped in silver, hanging from a leather string.

"Do you play chess?" I open.

"A little."

"You could be better than you think."

"Why do you say that?"

"You look chessish."

"Where's that?"

"Don't hustle me," I say, gesturing at my nose. "I've got a sandbagger detector."

I look down at the board, then up at her.

"Let's play."

"Oh, no, I don't play like you."

"You could learn."

"Besides," she says, "don't you want to finish your game?"

I speed the position, sacking down to a passed white rook pawn, the black king cutting off the white.

"Always move so fast?" she asks.

"Most of the time."

"Why?"

"Impatience."

"Can you see what happens?"

"Most of it. You see what you see."

"But you miss things."

"Sure, you miss things."

She laughs, the sound rippling out in a pair of four equal crests. "Is that wise?"

"Maybe it's not wise," I say. "But you miss things anyway. Though you could say you don't really *miss* what you didn't see."

"Don't you ever enjoy a leisurely game of chess?" she says, shaking her head, eyes crinkling.

"Slow chess is another game, but . . . if you've got the time."

"And the patience?"

I raise a white knight to her, as in toast. The pieces drop slowly one by one into their cloth sack, chink, chinkle; I tighten the string, fold the board, and place it back on the table. I'm not sure what's next. She's wearing a turquoise nylon runner's shell and spandex tights, so I try the Mayi Jogalong gambit.


Cynthia and I jog toward a lighthouse that will prove too far, since, after several miles, it hasn't gotten closer. Before the field work in Evora I've run once or twice a week since New York, mostly sticking the pack behind bushes on nice days and taking off for a half hour down the road, then returning, relief and saneness every time in finding the piled stones. We run on the roads for a while, then scramble down a steep scarp onto the beach. The firm red sand hurts my shins, splinted from walking the roads with my pack; two months after that steer, my ankle aches dully.

Cynthia's got a graceful, practiced, springy stride that swivels her slightly at the hips. She runs without notable breathing. For a few minutes I worry that she might, in fact, drag me to the lighthouse and back. We swap a few details about ourselves, a promising absence of *my boyfriend* talk on her part. There's just the sound of waves, our slight breathing, our sneakers printing the sand, as if talking would be an interruption, a pleasure in not hunting for words. High stone cliffs rise along the beach, the rock contorted and ribboned with veins of bright green chlorite. Cynthia's deep in some meditative groove. I try to run in sync with her, ease my way into the rhythm of her meditations, feel the loosening juice flow back into my legs after the runless days.

When we get back to the deserted beach below the hostel the sun is glancing over the green water. Cynthia unzips her shell and shakes out of her things, stretching her hamstrings gracefully, feet crossed and knees straight, muff visible when she bends. Then she skips naked to the surf, knee-deep and splashing, then diving through the spray, yelling at the impact of the first breakers.

"Come on," she yells.

We bodysurf a few big rolling waves, tensing at the icy water, and then swim out past the breakers to a large rock. Cynthia adjusts herself gingerly on the uneven, rough rock, shaking her hair, now clumped down about her shoulders. She shivers slightly in the chilly light, elbows seeking out a comfortable position on the rough stone behind her back, quartz crystal resting high on her breastbone.

Occasionally you have sharp flashforwards of the sort of person who will stun you when you meet. And when you meet, different as she proves from your fantasy, there's that shock of recognition. Though before you join the circus as a psychic, remember all the times these knowings went bust. I've kept believing that within the first minutes, after hearing a first laugh, seeing a few expressions, you know if you're interested. So I've known about Cynthia for an hour and a half.

When she laughs her eyes flicker closed and open with a shine; the laugh is laced with mirth.

"You have wistfulness in your laugh."

"Really?" she says, doing it again.

Gulls circle, screeching, then dive.

Though nothing in her body language gives me the green light my hands settle on her shoulders, massage her neck, and then move over her until I'm lightly cupping each breast, small, hard, defined; my lips press the back of her neck. Even as I'm touching her I can see that it's a potzer play, a ludicrous, laughingstock play. I want to slap my hands, tell them to heel. But, in chess parlance, *pièce touchée*. Once you touch a piece you've got to play it somewhere. Cynthia doesn't turn or act kissed. Chicken skin cold. My hands slip to her sides, then off.

"Joe Impatience," she says, exhaling slowly.

There's a light breeze. Though the sun is brighter, it's suddenly cooler on the rock; Cynthia crosses her arms over her breasts, wrings her hair, rubs her shoulders.

"I don't know," she says, with a different, almost inaudible, sandpapery laugh. She looks like she's silently rejecting a series of inexact ways to put something.

"I'm sorry," I say. "I wish there were someplace for me to crawl. I feel about an inch tall."

"It's probably just the cold water," she says.

I cross my legs.

# 7

"I worked in a restaurant once too," Cynthia says. "For about two hours. I was so terrible. My first customer asked me whether we had any salt and I asked if his girlfriend wanted some too. *Yes*, he said. *Salt for two*."

We sit on a large fine-sanded beach, crescent-shaped, enclosed by stone cliffs and grottoes flecked with the colored stone. Hour after hour, bronze Swedes and Germans, gleaming interchangeably with olive oil, perform Frisbee feats to make handkerchiefed mutts proud.

Around noon a group of French Earth People strum Simon and Garfunkel while the Swedes prepare lunch from their bags of practical cheeses and trail mixes, sitting in Yogic postures, slicing tiny pieces of cheese and applying them judiciously to Wasa breads. After a few bites, chewed with great earnestness, the Swedes signal how bloated they are, and strut around by the surf, bellies indeed slightly distended.

"Before Europe I accompanied this old widow to a condo in Saint Petersburg, Florida," Cynthia tells me. "Her husband had been an art tycoon."

"Besides being company," I ask, "what did you do?"

"Light spoon-feeding, tidying, and poem-reading," she says. "And I assisted the nurse, Mildred, in dressing the woman. I would read to the old woman—she was ninety—read poems written by her old friend Edna St. Vincent Millay. She would always say at the end, *Cynthia dear, that was so lovely, just lovely, my dear.* She had cancer which had spread. They stopped treatment, gave her six months. She would sit with two cardigans in the sun nodding herself to sleep. The whole thing was strange, but touching . . . you know. From the time I read to her she was legally blind, able only to recognize shapes. And she had this Southampton beach mansion—that's where I first read to her—full of de Koonings and Pollocks. Paintings she couldn't see. I stayed in Florida six months. She died, the old woman, a few weeks after she dove in the swimming pool."

"Did what?"

"Dove in the pool. I mean, I didn't think she could stand. I was reading in the sun and I fell asleep, book on my face, and woke to a chorus of old women screaming, *colored woman in pool, colored woman in pool.* I ran to the pool and saw the old woman flailing against the water. I swear. She was. By the time I'd reached the spot where she'd been, a couple of the nurses had her on the deck. When I got out of the water an immense black nurse, hair plastered on her face, was bent over the old lady, kissing and pumping the old woman back into temporary life."

She stops, looks out over the water.

"To think of that woman diving into the pool," she says, a smile-frown on her face.

Cynthia has been Eurailing around, seeing some sights. Though not too many lately, she adds; you can get monumented-out. She's not sure what she'll do after Europe, maybe move to Manhattan and work. For three mornings we run and swim together, and then go to the market, passing through the long clean fields, dotted with palm and olive trees, women in black spanking laundry with knotted sticks, the thwack-thwacks echoing like shotgun blasts. In the market stony old women, looking cast for the part, wrap kilos of fruit and cheese and fresh yogurt in white paper.

The night before she leaves we picnic overlooking what Cynthia now calls Granola Beach. We've decided to meet in a week in Seville. She'll train ahead to Algeciras, then wants to see the wild monkeys on Gibraltar. A sheer belvedere drops straight down to the sunlit sea, like we've rented a Port-a-Cupola. She's massaging my back, sun-oiled fingers working out the bunched feeling in my muscles and details about the home scene.

"Divorced, both remarried," I say. "Mom would like this beach. She's a vegan veggie, card-carrying co-opist."

"And your father?"

"He went Californian. Now we're like people who stay friends because they don't have to see each other often."


Before I left, Rick, my real father, and I ate at one of those restaurants that hurts when you're down. All glitter, happy chatter that excludes you. I bummed a cigarette and lit it with the bar candle, then put out the cigarette. The bartender organized glasses with unnecessary meticulousness and had a way of lifting them without spoiling the arrangement. I waited for Rick, drinking Vodka T's, wanting to be playing backgammon, to feel the night slide away in a low, tense key, to be one of the exhausted faces huddled around a board, following dancing dice into the next morning. Rick, east on business, wore a Hawaiian shirt, a lift in his stride, looking fit and tan.

"The worst stuff's regret," he said to me when the waitress had gone, leaning over the table with such a look of deliberation that no one could mistake the signs of a father giving crisis-council to his son.

"Don't get caught paralyzing yourself with what might have happened. Whatever happened happened."

There's a Slav-the-Bulgarian tightness to this point.

"What's the difference whose fault it was?" he continued, leaning so far over that his cheek practically wiped the lavender butter off my grilled salmon, then looking off in the waitress's direction as if his glance clinched some point. "You can't talk about fault, just compatibility. All those contracts are, you know, written in sand. You could love each other and not get along. You could love each other in different ways, at different times. It's all about lives that work together, just lives that encompass each other or don't."

"But how can you not regret the stupid things you do?" I asked.

"Everybody's stupid when they're in love. Love's probably just prolonged stupidity," he said, putting his hand on mine, then taking it off. "The illusion of continuance."

"You may be right," I said, though hovering over both of us were the words, *If anyone's an expert on this, you are.*

"How's your mom?" he asked, after a silence, an obligatory feel to the question.

"Fine," I say, an understatement. She and Tom, health maniacs both, married fifteen years, still hold hands everywhere, and must have a pact to get up and start dancing anywhere, anytime they hear "Born to Be Wild."


"I was into health food for a while," Cynthia says. "But I'd get these hallucinogenic cravings."

"For what?"

"Devil's food cake."

She's stopped rubbing my back, but I can still feel the warm tingle behind my neck.

"That was terrific," I say. "Let me give you one now."

"Absolutely not," she says. "My philosophy of back rubs is that only one person should give one on any occasion. That way it's more of an indulgence."

"But what if I want to give you a back rub?"

"When you're ready just pour me a glass of wine instead, please," she says.

She's brought a salad of red cabbage, bulgur wheat, cilantro, almonds, and lemon juice.

"If those clouds hurry up and intercept the sun," I say, looking off at a row of cruising strata, "we'll have ourselves a sunset, a mackerel sky."

We sit quietly, Cynthia sipping the white wine and looking out over the deserted beach. In the distance a few fishermen work snags out of their nets. There's nothing odd about not talking, just sharing the progress of the sunset. I work at the remaining salad, watching Cynthia's face, which does several things most of the time. She's a moody type, part of her sharp, animate, and droll, ready to leap into conversation, shaping words with her hands. Another part is distant, dreamy, reserved; she almost slides away from her words and has to hunt them back, find the departure point, remember she's with someone. She'll start saying something and then just stop, her mind drifting, an immersed haze in her face. Not at all like Julie, who is always emphatic, contentious, unpoker-faced, who can scowl while eating ice cream. Julie used to leave her car keys on bars so if someone said something dumb she could act like she'd been about to split.

Inadvertently, I mention Julie.

Cynthia asks if I'm a beach person, and we talk about beach times, and then a casual *we* slips out, and *we* grows into *we rented a beach house on Fire Island.* And then, aware of verging on psychobabble—hoping to seem sincere, though sincerity must always remain partial—I talk about busting up with Julie.

Behind us the sunset, uncomplicated by clouds, is evening into a luminous, deep glow.

"We don't have to talk about this," Cynthia says, the gentleness of her voice suggesting that rare ability to listen, to bring another's pain to oneself and so share in the disclosures empathy brings out.

When the sun and two bottles of wine are gone it's dark but still warm. A clear night. We walk holding hands. Cynthia's tipsy and skips us both along the road.

"You are a happy drunk, aren't you?" I say.

"Oh, yes, when I'm drunk I'm carefree. And cares are what make you unhappy."

In the distance the beams of the lighthouse sweep over the darkness in slow arcs.

"Tell me about some of your boyfriends," I say.

"Okay," she says, swallowing and scrunching her eyes in an amused grimace. She stops, nodding her head rapidly to a set of memories, laughs a little awkwardly. "My last real boyfriend was a professor, just divorced. He taught Environmental Politics."

I wait for the story to pick up energy and slide out, trying to be a good lubricant listener, like her, but half hoping the story has heartbreak in it too.

"I went to talk about a paper. God . . . there was a poster of the Statue of Liberty mostly underwater, just the torch sticking up like a buoy."

"Proceed."

"One night we went to dinner with an art-history teacher I'd studied Flemish landscape painting with. Brilliant woman, and so . . . well, just smashing. You know how there are those people you'd just like to be? The three of us ate in the Village one night, listened to jazz at the Blue Note. You like jazz?"

I nod, gesture her to continue.

"I kept thinking," she says, "here I am with her like a friend, unreal. I'd never felt noticed by her. I wouldn't have thought she knew my name. Then me and Jerry were driving back and we were talking about her . . . how this and that she was. . . . I was complimenting her . . . and he suddenly got silent, said he had to tell me they'd slept together that day. He'd been with his wife for eighteen years. He let me think about that. And now he was on his own again, and wasn't sure of his way. He hated that he'd been dishonest, but . . . I'm not boring you, am I?"

I shake my head vehemently, then slower. "Go on."

"I remember," she says, and she's got a bemused look, head shaking slightly, "I remember tears on his face in the lights of passing cars. He said he didn't want to break up, lose me entirely. What had happened didn't affect his feelings toward me. But he felt he'd want to see her again. At first I felt like asking him to let me out of the car."

Cynthia's stopped, let go of my hand.

"You . . . stayed in the car," I say.

"Yes." She laughs. "And the next thing he, or rather, they, wanted all three of us to be in . . . the car, together."

I take her hand again, aware of myself trying to gauge what the memory is taking her through, trying to get a fix on her, feel whether extending the car joke would be in order. She starts walking again, slowly, our hands swinging back and forth a little hard. An impulse to test her vulnerability, find the sore point, rises in me.

"Did you?" I ask.

"What?"

"Join them."

"Well," she says. She's stopped, hands on her hips, then

started walking again. "I couldn't believe she'd be attracted to me."

"Look," I say, stopping and putting on a reprimanding face. "That's something you really should believe."

"You guys," she says. "Nuts." She's shaking her head, swinging our hands harder, banging our hands against her thigh. I squeeze her hand, rotate my other hand to encourage the story.

"Why do you think I wouldn't, anyway?" she says, sounding vaguely annoyed. "Why do you assume. . . . Wait. Is it because of the other morning?"

I shake my head, mime a misunderstood wordlessness.

"Okay, you didn't say that. But you thought it, didn't you?"

"No, not really," I say.

"Well, I did join them, actually. Twice. So there."

We've stopped again. A starscape's come out, a nascent moon nearly full with a bright dog ring around it, the scent of blossoming orange and crange trees on the breeze. Neither of us says anything for half a minute; she's brooding; the mood seems altered, in danger of slipping away.

"If you must know," she says, nodding, "I was attracted to them, to her especially. It was all really confusing."

I can't think what to say to that. I'd like to say that whatever she did was fine and that everybody's confused, that it would be scary if you weren't confused.

"It made me feel empty," she says. "Cheap and diminished. Like I was their plaything."

We look at each other.

"I don't want to feel that way," she says, tears welling.

"Of course not," I say.

She smiles and shrugs almost apologetically, sniffles, and we hug. I stare out over her shoulder at the dark swells of the landscape, spreading palm trees, the large blank of the ocean. We're still hugging. I'm thinking, tears in my own eyes, aware that I'm half escaping into a soggy thought, that whatever generalizations you make refer to your own condition, that you never see the nature of people's confusion clearly, that their lives remain so unreal. We learn so little about where others are in the world.

"Come on," Cynthia says, pushing me away lightly, her memories almost visibly ebbing. "Enough of this, okay? Let's go for a dip."

# 8

After a week in Seville together, Cynthia and I arrange to meet at a youth hostel in Madrid. At first, alone on the road I'm glad for the solitude, the absence of planning, fitting schedules. But as days pass I find myself thinking of Cynthia, wondering where she is, what she's doing.

When I get in, the hostel is filled and the lights are out, so I check my sack, then wander into the bustling Plaza Puerta del Sol, which vibrates with celebratory energy. A train of people with their hands on one another's hips chugs by, drunk and gesturing others to join, yelling, "Venga, juntese a nosotros, viva, viva!" I catch hold of the end and snake through parting, cheering crowds. When the train busts apart I go to a *bodega* and eat oysters with onion and tomato, drinking Rioja Alavesa, and then crash for a few hours on a bench.

In the morning Cynthia and I visit the Prado. An American couple pays in front of us. When the woman opens her mouth there's a pause, then a nasal Midwestern twang. The man wears a Tyrolean outfit with lederhosen, and is sunburned over scabby sun blotches. Getting out of bed tomorrow for him will be like peeling adhesive tape from a wound.

"This man lacks an accordion," Cynthia whispers.

Inside, seven Japanese tourists obscure a large, angular, suffering El Greco saint. In between them you can glimpse gaunt supplicants, faces radiantly upturned against electric skies. The Japanese click away as if all is lost without physical proof, as if the photos are a receipt of presence. They photograph one another in every possible permutation, bowing among the El Grecos.

I hang back a few paintings behind Cynthia, and stay there, apace. It's always a sign of refinement to be able to stick it out longer in front of a painting. Like remaining seated until all the credits of a foreign movie have been shown. And trailing behind her I can both look at the paintings, watch the way she responds to them, or just watch her, the sashay and stop, the slope of her neck. She starts by looking at the canvas up close for a few minutes, then backpedals slowly, gazing intently; her eyes play along the motifs until, one hand on her hip, the other under her chin, the painting clicks open; she makes small, involuntary nods. There's an odd rise to thus watching her, a mixed sense that it's overly Italian to focus on women in a room filled with classic art—but foolish not to.

"Just too many paintings and people," Cynthia says, passing me where I'm seated on a bench. "There shouldn't be more than one painting to a room, on a blank wall, and they should let people in one at a time."

I'm seated across from *El Bufon Calabacillas*, one of a series of Velázquez portraits of the court jesters and dwarves of Philip IV, made for a gallery of figures of official fun. There's something disquieting, arresting, about the twisted mouths and foreshortened, stunted limbs: Sebastian de Morra, fists in his lap; Francisco Lezcano, eyes, lips, nose disfigured. El Primo sits with enormous folios on his lap, pen and ink cup at his feet, staring sternly at something beyond the viewer.

Next to me a fat American man has his shoes off and is rubbing his arches. He looks vanquished; his wife makes a garish show of ecstatic recognition, cooing like persons who converse with beribboned poodles. One look and I'm sure she makes a point of explaining every painting to him in details reaching far beyond the limits of his sustainable enthusiasm, deliberately, mercilessly, excruciatingly exacting a price for football season.

Don Juan de Calabazas, called Calabacillas, sits huddled in the corner of a bare room surrounded by pumpkins. His twisted fingers clasp one another on his lap. His eyes are glazed, almost glaucous and crossed; the painting blurs. At first I think I'm tired or have been looking at too many paintings or need glasses. Then it seems right that the painting is blurred, hazy. Perfect for the counterplotting, simmering shrewdness the fool has humped up under thousands of accreted abuses, years of derision. To the world he's a fool; what can he do but seem to laugh along, laugh at himself, plot quiet mischief, acknowledge that life requires several tactics? Any open retaliation from a fool only confirms the fool's status. So he shakes his bells, smiles enigmatically, bows and scrapes, offers his ass to the shoe, becomes addicted to an abuse that fixates him, makes him amplify every insult to himself. And inside he grows fisted, twisted, galled.

I've been looking at Calabacillas for about twenty minutes before I realize with a stunning embarrassment that I've been thinking about The Hallmark Card, whose squarish jaw I frequently dreamed of causing to be wired.


The last time I saw Julie she was with him. He had a perfectly vice-presidential, black brilliantined hairdo, and that protruding jaw. Hallmark and I took a tri-disciplinary seminar together: Economics, Politics, and Literature of the American Thirties.

He always looked like he'd walked straight out of a barbershop for Young Republican toastmasters, and seemed the sort who spent every waking moment trying to appear more than he was.

She had come over to get a few last things at a time when I was usually working at the restaurant. I saw the elevator closing and yelled "hold that sucker" and jumped through the doors before I realized it was them. When she saw me get in the elevator she gave his hand a little squeeze. There's a fine line between carelessness and maliciousness. Her normally straight hair was done up as if an architect had planned it and just removed the scaffolding. They wore identical knee-length gray overcoats and bright scarves, looking like they'd stepped out from a fraternity semiformal.

"Somebody say something," Hallmark says, and shuffles his feet. He's got an insolent expression, now uneasily supercilious, as if he's run into his yacht club valet after hours.

I'm wearing a sweatshirt Julie gave me that once belonged to a former boyfriend of hers, so I say to him, "You ought to wear this now, like the yellow jersey in the Tour de France."

He laughs a little sickly, gives her a supportive look.

"Keep your shirt on," Julie says, eyebrows rising in annoyed inverted vees that weaken my legs.

I fix on the green dot highlighting the ascending numbers. Each floor takes minutes, though we do not stop. Once Julie and I stopped the elevator between floors late at night and made love, the elevator shaking, our backsides alternately mashing all the buttons the way morons do for kicks, until some bastard yanked the alarm. I want to ask if she remembers this. My head buzzes with the remnants of assorted, layered hangovers.

Julie uses her key and marches right into the apartment to get the boxes, overcoat rustling over her legs, me fixed in the doorway as he walks by with a little shrug and she hands him a box. Then she puts the key on the dresser we refinished together and walks out and presses the elevator switch.

"Christ, get some sleep, Jason," she says. "You look like a raccoon."

For the first time since Italy these and associated memories come at me, too unexpected and distant to hurt. I sit staring at Calabacillas, nodding, remembering a lunch two weeks after Julie hashed me, after which my intervention in a domestic dispute involved sticking up a Mexican without a gun.

Julie had started as a Wall Street paralegal and instead of answering my questions on the phone slipped in bits about memorizing the contents of boxes. I sat down at her desk, taking in the familiar tear-off dictionary calendar, looking at notes she'd written herself and arranged neatly on the leather writing mat I bought her. Then my eye was drawn to this poem, written in felt pen and ringed by the sort of three-color flair design kindergartners do for homework at posh schools:

> For me it is not a question whether
> You want to settle down with me
> Because when we are together
> I feel very lucky
>
> So if we should
> Last just a little while
> For me it will have been good
> If it leaves you with your smile.

There was a rose next to it in one of those junior-size carafes. The last time I'd offered her a rose she snatched it out of my hand and stomped on it. For moments I sat too stunned to be ashamed of myself for having read his sappy doggerel.

"Let's go, Jason," she said, looking around, as if scared that, standing there in my restaurant penguin suit, I'd start in on her romance of the rose-poem and make a scene, and people would think she'd had liaisons with the sandwich delivery man.

"What can I get youse two?" asked the waiter of the glorified pizza shop where we ate.

When I looked into her eyes it was too obviously an interview. Forced and flat, everything affected. The bereaved ex's hearing. She was irretrievably gone and resented me for dragging her away from her improved life to the peripheries of my pain and delusions, resented me for parading around like a mirror of her unconcern. Nobody likes to be suffered over when they've changed the channel. People want to think you're feeling whatever they're feeling and that if they're okay you must be too.

"What was it really?" I say. "Was it the gambling?"

"You can't make a shopping list of reasons," she said, haltingly in that never-finish-a-sentence mode of hers, like my state was cramping her candor, making her words torture, the way gin players lift a card, stare into space, push the card back down into the hand, then tug at a different one. "Sure . . . I didn't like the gambling . . ."

And I sat back listening to the surgical comments, knowing even before she chopped them with her Chief-Arms-Negotiator logic that my grievances were pathetic: "you're . . . but . . . but . . . you must know. . . . I . . . we . . . could never." Comments to be prized open later when, feeling like a hydrant in a dog pound, I'd jog slowly uptown, knocking my head for the way I'd garbled everything, for the crowds of misshapen phrases limping out of my unhinged mouth. I needed to see her point of view. Yes, I would think, on that jog—bow tie on lapel, around Central Park—yes, everyone wants to record an album of themselves singing in the shower. What's sad is when you think other people enjoy the crooning sounds you make. For her it's simply not an important failure. I believed in love, she said, and she loved that in principle. But she wanted to be happy right away, love, principle, or not. And she just wasn't happy with me. We needed to get on with our lives, she said. Maybe later we could be friends.

"Jason," she said, "we fought a lot. Remember that, okay? You're idealizing the shit out of me and what we had. I don't want to be idealized. I'm just me."

"You're a deep and lovely person," I, Calabacillas, said.

"This on-all-fours romantic routine is too much to stomach. Just stop it, okay. Just chill."


When Cynthia's train pulls out two days later I'm still annoyed at my thoughts in the Prado. They're like a hangover involving memories of hangovers. I'm irked by the fact of having been popped out of those memories by Cynthia's hand on mine. She said, giving me that eerie feeling that she'd been reading my thoughts, that it was dangerous to stare into the faces of buffoons too long, and that I ought to look at happy painters. So we walked to the Tiepelos.

Now I wander the terminal feeling dazed, wishing Cynthia and I had shared more intimacy, though we've had good talks and have arranged to meet again in a few days. Suddenly I crave a meal, but avert my eyes from vendors and the cream-filled tarts in the newspaper kiosks. There's always the impulse to overeat out of fear of starving later; then you hike around bloated in the sun, like roadkill.

It's a clear, crisp afternoon, road fresh as after a rain. I walk for a while, sun starting to sink, thinking of Cynthia rattling across the plains toward Barcelona, hopeful that she is thinking of me. A car speeds by and I wheel too slowly to get eye contact. The past mornings I've woken full of expectancy, anticipating our jogs, and even the sight-seeing, yet irritated. We've only really kissed a few times, yesterday overlooking Toledo, and that last night in Sagres, shivering against each other knee-high in the surf, me awaiting a sign, some shift toward another stage, my mind starting with Kama Sutra imaginings of us tangled: She's bronzing on our rock in the sun, her stomach spray-beaded, glistening, and I've placed my index finger in her and started a very slow stroke, sliding back and forth. There's a faint smile on her face, like she's holding up under the opening moments of a tickle attack, like she's not as far off in the high sun haze, as closed eyes, still lashes want to indicate. And as I move my finger she begins to roll and move in unison, in little waves, a growing arch in her back, her buttocks starting to clench and release.

Question: Are all of us fundamentally sleazes, or are these fancies of Cynthia lust for the unobtained or defenses against Julie? What was it about Julie, anyway? The emotional autopsy begins, that cross-examination and aimless picking apart and dividing of questions into transparently false either/or's between which to twist. Was it all vanities and delusions, the pleasure of heads turning at our hand-holding? Can I fall out of love just because she loves me not, if she ever did? Do I, as Julie said, *believe*, if only because, whatever pathologies beliefs come from, however much belief and capacity differ, when you don't stay open to love, what will you do?

Around dusk a car with a French license—end digits suggesting Nice—stops and I trot up half-reluctantly, as if the lift's interrupting thoughts I'm chin deep in. I answer a few questions. He says that he works in the Bibliothèque Nationale so many times that I'm sure he doesn't work there. "Oh là là," he says when we pass a structure. "J'aime les images, toutes les images, les formes." He yawns. I offer to drive. Behind the wheel, I shift into drive, road hum becoming inaudible, like riversound. Soon he's asleep, head pressed against the window, snoring lightly, occasional catchings of breath. It darkens slowly, the road-stars that string out along tight dividing lane-lines gradually emerging. I'll wake the driver for gas, and again at the border.

Before Julie I'd always had the sense, too late, of running from feeling, then wondering why I'd never really given it a shot, whether it was in me to sustain a relationship, to abandon myself to the requisite degree. So the main investments weren't made, affairs fizzled into tacit agreements—no plates thrown—that we each had a lot to offer someone else, every relationship enforcing a sense that if what it was all about was finding someone with whom you can roll out of bed time and again with sticky optimistic mouths and hair disarrayed to say hello world then I was so far up a creek that a paddle wouldn't help.

One night after troubles started with Julie, Fred and I sipped in the closed bar until the streets started getting gray and then went to his house and cooked dinner for us, and breakfast for his wife and his three-year-old. We let ourselves in, shushing each other.

"There's some things you seem to want to miss," Fred whispered earnestly in the kitchen. We were sautéeing onions, garlic, in one pan in preparation for poaching a steak in red wine.

"Sample this," Fred said, pouring me something he'd been mixing. "My potation. And make yourself useful. Can you whisk an egg, man?"

I shook my head sadly.

"Figures you can't. Cut these up."

I diced up some tomatoes and green peppers. He slid the vegetables onto a sizzling pan. The bacon met the crackling mix with an extended *shuuush*.

"Look, it ain't about a weekend. And nobody just gets along. Holding it together's work. Like a job."

"A person's not a job," I whispered back.

"Hell, yes, every person's a job, man, a project," he said, whisper almost cracking. "And one way or the other, if you want to hold a steady job you got to take a pay cut."

"I just can't figure us," I say.

"Listen, man. You dig this woman because she's into different things than you. . . . You're not really like her. Half of your sad ass wants to be converted, to reject what you are. The other half's just into preppie blowjobs."

"One question," I sputtered.

Fred nodded.

"The fuck's in this . . . drink?"

"What's that I smell?" Fred's wife asked, rubbing her eyes, hair tousled, sniffing bacon and steak fumes. Both of us jumped at her sudden entrance. I'd only met her a few times. "Freddie, are you poisoning our guests again with those . . . shakes?"

Then the kid toddled in, threw a couple of infant punches at Fred, tripped, and Fred scooped him up, saying, "Hey, Champ, easy now."

Fred hugged his wife, her cheek pressed to his; his kid climbed over his broad shoulder. I shook my head, then held my hands up as if clicking a family portrait.

"You guys look like a black Norman Rockwell," I said. "Really now, honestly. How's married life?"

They shrugged and smiled.

"You want to crash in the Champ's crib, Jason?" Fred asked after breakfast, about to leave for a morning business class.


Could Julie have loved me beyond those moments thrill-seekers share?

Our silences got longer. We'd walk down the street without talking, an awkwardness about not having anything to say, me knowing she expected good, clever repartee and considered a person without *conversational resourcefulness* bankrupt, but me also feeling a defiant urge not to talk, if, in fact, I could think of anything witty through my annoyance at the demand.

If I'd put on a power-tie with a horsehair shirt underneath, sat in subways with my face at the level of midgets' armpits, quit the gambling, subscribed to a flower plan, wrote rhyming poems. . . . Or is there just something distancing and flat in me, some transparent reaching after conditions I'm constitutionally incapable of? Must I always be a spectator at events in my own life that I can't prevent? Must I always miss the clear response to the particular fix of the moment?

There's still the thought of Julie, the contours of her face, features distinct, the tightness and yet smooth softness of her skin into which she nightly massaged Parisian moistening creams, that face all a lure, in other faces, even in Cynthia's, eerie traces of hers, that face, still warping variations of itself onto the ruffled screen of my imagination against my will. There's the view of her from behind as she washes dishes or strokes her long black hair fifty times in the morning or night, sitting cross-legged in lamplight on our futon. There's the smoothness of Julie's long legs, those legs that keep going, the pleasure to the point of arousal I get from hearing her laugh, her mouth open with surprise and delight, held open cartoonishly wide and long, then breaths cascading out, her lips on a pen from across the library (we always remember the cheap stuff). Images of her spontaneities mixed with the sense of her unreasonableness, her blackboard present-tenseness, her like-o-graphic memory: what she likes she remembers, what she doesn't, she just wipes off.

There's her passing me a note, ballpoint on monogrammed napkin, to meet her in the ladies' room at the Phi Beta Kappa dinner and, mostly, that sense of how, hearing the written words as she would have whispered them—Bergman-throatily, *knock twice and don't you dare keep me waiting*—and watching her impossibly thin waist sway, knowing she exaggerated that sway because she knew I'd ache watching, the sense of how, excusing myself after a painful and I hoped convincing interval from the provost, who strung together an astonishing sequence of sports metaphors, and who felt this event was the Sugar Bowl of his academic season and laughed at frankly unfunny jokes with an accuracy painful to hear, the sense of how, imagining just how fast Julie would lock that ladies' room door behind us, I felt for the first time in my life, truly, no doubt undeservedly, but positively blessed.

# 9

Zooming along the road sometimes I want to open the car door and drag one foot out, sharpening my foot into a stump of penciled bone like a knife on a grindstone. First my Converse goes, then skin. I can see my foot filed off and dust leaping sparklike from the bone and yes, plenty of blood. I remember the amputation scene from *Gone With the Wind* where a man is strapped to a dining table. A doctor enters the tent with a hacksaw and a lantern. He sets the lantern down and draws the curtain across the screen.

Outside Lyons an open cream Cadillac slows to a stop through wavering heat haze, dust rising by the road.

"Merci," I say, when I've trotted up to it.

"Marcy," the driver says. "Save your French and throw your sack in back."

I jump in back with two guys; in the front there are two girls besides Marcy, hair blown over their shoulders, both reclining into the sun with looks of fixed indifference, like the auto-maidens in Rick's designer blue jean ads. Almost immediately we're doing 150 kilometers. A herd of white Charolais cows staring off over a rocky field whiz by, and some goats.

"Friends call me Surface," one of the guys yells into the wind. He's black, immaculately dressed in a three-piece suit and dark mirror glasses, a red silk handkerchief dotted in the breast pocket of a suit navy blue, a suede cowboy hat on his lap. "My main man here's Timothy Warren Stenton III."

"My associates call me Stunts," says Stenton.

His hair's severely cropped, and he wears a camouflage suit and high black army boots, pants tucked, an excessively large ribbed knife on his belt, something hunted in his eyes. He gives me a cowhand's handshake, his forearm unnaturally knotted, looking like a samurai making a statement in a rodeo. I feel like bowing and scratching.

Marcy's hair is braided and then pinned up behind her head.

"You look too much like an old boyfriend of mine," she says over her shoulder.

"Maybe I should get out here, then," I say.

"Naw, stick around," she says, winking. "But don't make me get out my whip."

We pull to a stop by the road. Marcy jumps out and holds up her dress around her in one hand. A burnt crescent of skin shows at her midriff. Angélique and Emma sit on the edge of the car door. They still haven't turned my way. The grass hisses below Marcy.

"Don't stare so hard," she says, rolling her eyes at Stunts.

"It's just wine," Stunts says. "Ain't nothing wrong with looking at a 1985 Merlot-Blanc, such as it was."

"You wish it were wine," she says, winking at Surface.

Surface says they're with the orchestra of the musical extravaganza *The One-Armed Swimmer*, winner of two Tonys, heading from Lyons into a week's run in Paris. After that they have a month before meeting up in Tokyo.

"During that month we plan to reconnoiter some," he says. "If you catch my meaning."

"All month," Surface says. "Until we need some of those geisha mermaids in a Jacuzzi to make us right."

"Got Japan on my mind," Stunts says, shooting me an adversarial look, something discomforting in its transparent aggressiveness.

"Yes, Stunts-san. Yes," Surface says.

"Well," I say to Surface, turning to avoid Stunts's look. "Kemo-sabe here won't need a haircut."

Surface guffaws, throws his head back into the wind, slaps his knee.

"Let's extend an invitation to Slick, here," Stunts says.

"Slick, you're invited," Surface says, still laughing deeply.

"I'll make a note of the invitation," I say.


In Paris we go straight to Le Café Cluny. Marcy lets us out and goes to park. We pull together two tables outdoors. When the waiter comes Stunts orders three bottles of merlot and a quart of mescal tequila, essence of agave in the worm.

We all raise our shot glasses.

"Yo," Stunts says.

I gambled in Atlantis next to a man who'd yell, "Yo 'leven" on every come-out roll and then, "Yo mama, yo mama," laughing himself into a hoarse frenzy. Everyone started yelling with him, including a man who held his chips in an artificial metal arm, taking them out with his good hand to bet, and I found myself yelling, "Yo mama," too. And then looking around in an odd, flushed moment, feeling suddenly detached from the lurid, hungry faces, but knowing I'd been every bit as involved as each, my frenzied shouts going out with theirs, tied temporarily to them all in a moment of coincident self-interest but essentially isolated, feeling with sudden acuteness their intense streakish loyalties. The hot crap-table loyalty that dies when the dice stop dancing, freeze. And every player's alone, feeling that boredom but still not quite dulled edge of possible reversals that keeps excluding nonplaying options.

Stunts pours one in my glass, fills his.

We tank them. Squeeze lime.

He pours another, raises his glass.

"Alterations," he says.

The old rush loosens my veins.

Under my jean jacket I'm wearing a 10K shirt that says CHASE ME. Stunts gazes at it with more and more intent, shaking his head as if he can't quite make it out, his grin like that of the chronic malfeasant who starts with a blowgun in kindergarten. The haircut's a fierce antagonistic thing on an American, worse than a shaved head, like he might cut off someone else's ear. Something compelling in his look.

"I'll bet you've never been to a pig-picking, Slick," Stunts says, forehead practically touching mine, his voice matter-of-fact. "You've got New York candy-ass all over your face."

"Don't tell me where you're from," I say. "I know I've never heard of it."

"And by the way," Stunts says, leaning over as if confiding in me, "if you wear a shirt like that someone's going to call your bluff."

"That there sounds to me like challenging words," I say in as dopey a drawl as I can.

"Slick, you ever gamble?"

"I turn over a card now and then."

"Ever put your money where your mouth is?"

"When I'm holding."

"And you ain't holding. Nothing but that knockabout rucksack on your back."

"That's right."

"That some kick you're on."

"We get our kicks how we can, right?" I say.

"Five hundred says my kick's better 'n yours, you slick-ass Siddhartha motherfucker. Five C-notes says you can't lick me in no race."

"Save your money for worthy causes," I say, but already there's a hum in my head and my legs are getting that itch under the table, trying to gauge the stiffness from the walking, feel the spring, remember the last hard run.

"Five hundred against what?" I say.

"Your pride, if you've got any."

I spread my hands.

"Humor me. I'm rich," says Stunts.

"He's rich," Surface says. "I'd advise you to humor him."

"Got more money than time," Stunts says, and lights a hundred. B.F. Goodrich's face burns with an orange-and-black curl, a vaguely nauseating sight after my scrimpy strings of three-dollar–sausage-and-cheese days.

"Well," I say. "Now wasn't that stupid."

"You want a hundred?"

"I don't want your money."

"Then what do you care what I do with mine, Slick?"

He stands up and stretches a few times.

"Take off your shoes, Siddhartha," Stunts says. "If you're not used to it, you should start getting used to it."

"You're faded," I say.

Marcy's just come back. She sits on Surface's lap and he hands her one full bottle.

"You boys watch out for glass," she says, drinking straight from the merlot.


We jog across the street, passing fire-eaters, sword swallowers, a man dancing in front of an open café to the music of a hand-held tape recorder. An old Arab with feet splayed inside out like reverse Charlie Chaplin legs cries cubed sweets on a tray. We pass Odéon, heading at a slow pace toward the park, bare feet stinging on the pavement.

At the gate to the park, locked, we strip off our shirts and begin stretching, silent.

"How far's it around?" Stunts says.

"Mile and a half, maybe," I say, having run it several times when I stayed with Yvonne. The inside loop is slightly longer, winding through the gardens, chess players, fountains, movable crêpe stands. If she shows, Cynthia and I will make that loop our morning run.

I lie on my back and put my legs over my head, pushing the stiffness of my back out through the toes, feeling the old cross-country anticipatory rush, immediately seeing runs by our wind-ripped, white-capped lake, spray leaping from a bank of stone in icy gusts, lashing to break my stride, pierce my sweats and make me turn round, coast back across the frozen ground, and I hear our old hunchbacked Coach Black calling us together, *huddle up boys, hands together now*, sleet stinging our just-bared arms, lobstering our thighs. *Listen up, boys, here's the plan*, a nearly comic intensity stretching his face as he gives us the familiar plan: *Go out hard, work the middle, bring it home strong*. And we're trotting to the starting line.

I work the inside of my legs and hamstrings with hurdler stretches, then get up.

"You through aerobicizing?" Stunts says.

"Let's do this," I say.

And immediately we're running hard, locating the gait, the pounding of pavement on the balls of my bare feet like being hit with a stick; we're dodging traffic from Boulevard Saint-Michel and then opening up on a quiet, dark stretch. I figure I won't mess with him and run as hard as I can hold, calculating the distance and the time, trying to achieve the concentration, apply pressure, make the kind of gap that widens, busts his will, grows into a bounded space when the contact gets lost. Then when I've got a few yards I try to bury him, cranking the shift, remembering how in college we watched reruns of the ageless Ethiopian Yifter the Shifter and yelled *Stick-Shift and Burn* before Indian-file surges in training. Yifter would take off as on a musical cue and just glide, like he was about to ascend. But I can't quite shake Stunts. Surprising. A dull, hot pain starts through my feet and into my shins. The bars of the gate whip by like bike spokes. Crank on him, I think. Come on. Shift gears on the bastard.

But at about a mile he surges even, though laboring, and we run stride for stride, breathing hard, dodging the random pedestrian. He ups the pace again and I just hold contact, feeling my breath going, concentrating on the center of his back as we near the top end of the park, lights of Rue de Vaugirard blurs of red and green, a confusion of raining colors, and bank into the final quarter. At about the same moment we both rise on our feet, changing the center of charge into the chest, and start jugular racing. Air rushes through me and spears my lungs and lifts me woozy and gasping and feet all on fire off the ground. My arms flap wildly, head moving side to side, buildings outside the park whizzing, traffic lights by the darker park whipping by, pressing us away into the sprint, flying uncontrollably forward and desperately. We make a sharp turn and see the shirts maybe two hundred yards off and it's home stretch and kick, finish-line consciousness, reach for the beach, only the rasping of breath and whistling away of trees and the absurd speed of pavement catching up below. An unbelievable heaviness in the thighs, thereness, pain concretized into a kind of lurching clarity. I've opened a few yards but everything's moving slow, the bear on my back, shoulder blades pulling back, absolute rigor mortis setting in. I'm staggering, fighting to stay erect, and then behind me there's a crash and I'm by the shirts and I turn and see a body bounding and skidding, flipping over, hands out, flipping out, an eerie slowness and dreaminess about it all as Stunts bodysurfs along the pavement.

I sink to my knees and lie on the ground. My heart beats furiously and there's a razor sharpness through my shoulders. My head goes blank and then opens and closes. I'm still flat on the ground. A woman in a shawl comes and kneels by me and starts prodding my shoulder to see if I'm okay. A small crowd surrounds me, chattering, obscuring my view. Faces lean in and now, gradually, I can make out some of the words. . . . *Comment vont-ils?* . . . *C'était une course.*

"Okay, okay," I say, and pull myself up. My feet are blister burned: blood trickles between my first and second toes. I inspect my toes. Okay. Nothing significant. An old man, tremendously excited, keeps slapping me on the back, raising my arm, repeating *le champion, le champion, quelle course* in a way that makes it hard to know if he's joking, or whether if he happened to be carrying wreaths I'd be heavily bedecked.

"Pas de problème," I keep saying, still trying to measure my breath while the man thumps my back.

Stunts leans over a car, his uniform torn and the skin below his knees barked orange-red.

"Stunts," I call.

A car zooms past in the street. Then another. The people disperse. We're alone again.

"Stunts?"

I pick up our shirts, stabilize myself on a car, walk over to Stunts, lean against the car and hand him his shirt.


"You win round one," Stunts says, nodding his head. We're back at the tables. "Here's that five."

I start to refuse and then, looking at the hilarity in his face and at the green on the table, just fold and pocket the cash.

Later I'll stick it under the lining of my sneaker, keep it intact in case I wind up facing a casino with the urge. Then I'll go double or bust a few hands with it.

"Have a nightcap," Stunts says.

The end of the tequila makes my gums water. Stunts offers me the guave. I bite half off, give him the other. Brotherhood of the worm.

"Catch the O.A.S.," Surface says, handing me a bunch of theater tickets to their show. I stare at the extras.

"Case you luck into company."

"Scalp 'em if you want," Stunts says.

There's the silence within street noise; tonight's action seems played out, not worth forcing out of tedium or following into escalations. I sling my sack over my shoulder.

"Got plans, eh, Slick?" Stunts says.

"Big ones."

"Blah, blah, blah," Stunts says, opening and closing one hand to indicate babbling.

"See that you get a Band-aid for that leg," I say.

# 10

The streets are nearly empty at 6:00 A.M. An old smocked woman goes by with a cart of baguettes. You offer a few francs for one and she gives it to you, refuses the money vehemently, spits. A man sweeps the streets in front of his Rotisserie with a broom made of sticks. A scrawny kid unstacks tables outside a bistro. By a hydrant there's a lake of vomit. You walk through the rose-tinted buildings and the gray streets smelling bread and chewing slowly on your own, and you exchange "bonjours" with the hookers in the doorways. The beat-up sack and three-day dirt and half-eaten baguette give you license to salute without buying. There's a woman with dark mirror glasses and a spike bracelet holding a kitten. You smile, and she looks at you like an older sister. Hello, Sister, morning to you and may a juicy nondrinking, reflex-protecting, Four Star, Gold Card—carrying American aircraft-carrier fighter pilot glide gently down your landing strip.

I change, shave, and wash thoroughly in the McDonald's, sunbathe for a few hours in the Jardin des Tuileries, read the *Herald*

*Tribune* and work the crossword, then weave through the tight streets of St.-Michel, craving a *tarte fraise*, in the mood for food—a bowl of almost flammable Moroccan red sauce poured over a platter of sliced lamb and grease-soaked *pommes frites*. The windows are cornucopias: tarts and puddings, a glazed apricot cake lightly dusted with powdered sugar, a shrimp and scallop kabob in a Tunisian restaurant, resting on the plate of a man who shaves sections off it, engrossed in every bite until he catches sight of me drooling and motions me away. I want to cultivate my appetite for a dinner with Cynthia, and if I break down and snack the monkey off my back I'll eat myself into a stupor. At a few minutes to two I'm headed for the Place St.-Michel, seeking Cynthia.

Around the fountain, drunk Moroccans strum guitars and whistle after Swedish girls on that thousand-to-one chance. A tape deck blares Arabic music that sounds like a radio tuned to four different stations at once. The shallow water is ashen, filled with bottles, filters, dissolving butts. While I'm waiting a man in a long plaid jacket climbs the statue of St. Michel and sits on the saint's head. By the time he's reached the head of the statue he has a crowd. Looking down at the fountain and his cheering supporters, he draws a bag out of his coat and begins to eat chicken, bringing the meat to his mouth in dramatic, sweeping arcs. When two police arrive and order him down, one whistling through his fingers, the man laughs and waves them away with a drumstick, sitting cross-legged on the saint so it seems the statue has two heads. The man takes salt and pepper packets from his pocket and seasons the meat to taste, daubing his lips with a pocket handkerchief after every bite.

They counsel, then one policeman throws a rope over St. Michel's arms and scales the statue quickly. The man gets off the head politely and stands on the saint's shoulder, setting his food down on the wavy bronze hair. For lack of anything better to do the officer stands across from him on the other shoulder and tries to persuade the fellow to descend. The smell of the chicken seems to distract the cop, and the man offers him a piece. The policeman knocks the chicken into the crowd, which follows the arc of the drumstick, then hisses emphatically.

Waiting by the road is one thing. You relax; it might be all day. Waiting for a late person is another. You swing through ranges of thoughts and emotions. The clock strikes two-fifteen and then two-thirty. Still no Cynthia. I haven't considered a no-show, or that I might not see her again. As the minutes slide away I hope she's okay and hasn't forgotten the time/place, since we made no Plan B. I sit, cross-legged, blood pounding in my ears, waiting for her with that dropping-away-of-your-gut feeling that you get when you overbet a hand. You know you're committed to gambling what you can't afford, but can't pull back. You're two-paired and rate a pair out there and you shove all-in thinking how if you don't fill the boat you can bluff the hand. What an exquisite feeling when you turn up the edge of that slid down-card, not letting your face tell though inside you're ringing.

I sit as still as I can, trying to empty my mind of thoughts like you do when you're bluffing, having a transcendental moment, or trying to diet. One spiritual self-help manual recommends thinking, waiting, and fasting as roads to self-improvement. At times, fishing or hitching, I feel I'm progressing along two of these roads. Clearly, I don't fast well. And even doubt fasting as a ramp onto the true highway. Now I could eat with Mange-tout, the Frenchman who ate a bike in one sitting. In an interview, he said the saddle tasted best. Could Nirvana, freedom from hunger, really be worth it?

I'm there for three-quarters of an hour. The more I wait, at once irritated and concerned, the more I swing between images of disasters—her train twisted under a bridge, a bomb in a McDonald's—and images of us walking, running, sunbathing on the beach. Since we've made no declarations, staked no claims, can't Cynthia have been waylaid, or skinny-dipped else-where? I think of her easiness with nakedness, and wonder if it's Europeanness, maturity, tease, or confusion. And as always, at the moment when you most mentally malign someone, she shows up, and the sight of her at the edge of the *place* fills me with a glad relief. She's wearing a jean jacket and has a yellow handkerchief tied around her neck, and she's got on one of those shoulder string purses thieves have wet dreams about. I wave, but she doesn't see me, and then, catching sight of me and waving back, she trots across the square, momentarily hidden between walkers, and I rise to walk toward her.

We eat a few *crêpes confitures* and then stroll through the Lux-embourg Gardens arm in arm, passing the fountain where women watch their boys prodding their sailing boats, and men gaze over the tops of their sunglasses and books at the women, and we wander along paths fringed by straight rows of horse chestnut trees, passing old men who squat to pitch *boules*. Far-ther on, fringing a garden, are the stone chess tables. Small groups huddle around speed games; students work positions out of a book.

"You're pretty hot at chess solitaire," Cynthia says. "Let's see how you do against people."

"Watching couldn't be much fun," I say.

"I could watch a few games, go ahead."

"I always wanted to play chess in Paris," I say, while waiting for a board. "In grade school I imagined dim cafés where men played in dark glasses and berets. I'd walk into a café and sit across from one of them. Without speaking he'd make his move, and I'd put on my shades and say, *Now I can't see the board either.* But I've never met a player with dark glasses who didn't stink, and anyone wearing a beret is automatically funny."

"You must find Paris hilarious," she says.

I sit down across from a middle-aged man who's got wads of paper in his shirt pocket along with assorted pens and pencils. He hardly looks at me when I sit down, but holds his two fists way out in front of the board. I pick black and we set quickly. He opens with queen four, and, tipping my hat toward West Seventy-second, I reply with the Slavic defense, blood rising, instant heat at the temples, our hands in alternate rhythm mashing the levers on the clock. After a few moves the position tangles, knights awkwardly centralized and entrenched. We're playing three minute and the vectors open and clench; I catch a glance of Cynthia watching, try to smile, and then put my hands to my forehead like blinders, concentrating into the position so there's just the board and the pulse of the game. I get a slight advantage but can't finish, and feel flushed and cramped for time, moving too fast, frustrated at my inability to find the crack in his lines, resorting to obvious tricks until I've lost my edge and must fight not to lose. He staves off my attack, parries ineffectively, not quite finding his counterattack and then, glancing at the clocks, sacks down to a knight-king no-win. No mating material. A draw. We reset quickly, hands almost colliding, mutually annoyed and not looking at each other. He tilts the clock toward me. I nod. We split the next two, both book through ten moves. The man's head doesn't rise when I leave. We haven't exchanged a word. He mutters something to himself, evens out the clock levers to stop the ticking, and writes a note on one of the clumps of paper. Someone quickly takes my seat.

After chess there's numbness, games on the brain. You don't want to talk. You want to close your eyes and review the sequences like practice films in slow motion, probing after that first rift where your opponent set the wedge, worked, widened, and your game fell apart.

Cynthia and I walk along the Pont Neuf, passing the statue of someone who was triumphant enough or had enough of the right connections to have his exploits commemorated in bronze, a dignified green man on his rearing horse, now ingloriously weather-stained and spattered with pigeon shit. The streaked sky reminds me of streusel, sugar-glazed. Large lamps blink on overhead, sending our shadows faintly in front of us. Below on the banks old fishermen hold long *goujon* poles. Tom would check what they're using, the test of the line, the power-weight ratio of the shaft. We stand watching the light on the buildings across the river; the windows gleam tiny rectangles of orange, then dull quickly. The lamps on the bridge click on; in a few more minutes it's dark.

"Over here," Cynthia says, climbing over the thick wall that overlooks the water on a wide cement ledge.

"Careful," I say. "You sure it's okay?"

"It's fine."

"Doesn't look wide enough."

"Don't be a chicken, come on."

I ease myself over gently. Someone's eaten cherries where we sit, and we brush the pits into the water, listening carefully for the splash but not hearing it. We're hanging over the water, legs dangling; it takes a minute to adjust to the height, another minute to look out over the river, now a dark, dirty green curve of road. To the right the Ile de la Cité ends abruptly in a cluster of trees and benches, and far behind there's the huge illuminated sign for Samaritaine. To the left vague shapes of parked barges and riverboats, outlined by strings of light, hug the banks. Ahead, flooded by lights, the palace of the Louvre rises, squarish towers white in the glare, traffic on the bridge, cars going places. I take Cynthia's hand and we stare out over the water.

"Did you miss me?" she asks, after a few silent minutes.

"I was scared you wouldn't show."

"Why would you think that?"

"Because I missed you, I guess," I say, and kiss her cheek.

"I thought about you, too," she whispers, twisting so my next kiss grazes her. "Just chill."

She puts her hands on my chest as if to shove me.

"You wouldn't."

"Oh, no?"

I move to kiss her again but she keeps me away.

"Careful," I say. "It's a long way down."

"Then don't go overboard."

"Cynthia," I say. "I can't swim."

"You could in Sagres."

I close my eyes, picture us kissing in Sagres under that bright moon, the two of us bursting into wolf calls. She starts to move toward me, puckering her lips with a mischievous look, her hands still on my chest. Then, just when I think we're about to kiss, my direction reverses. She's pushed me hard and I'm speeding away from her lips, slow and then faster, suddenly aware of whooshing air, weird free space falling away from the bridge, a panic ending with the smash of water and a new panic. The water has rushed up and connected, spray shivering up around, and I've shot through it into a thick blackness, a scary depth. I struggle upward through the dark, the moment interminable, and burst the surface to look around. On the bank: a confusion of colored lights. I spit out a mouthful of water. The current is sweeping me, moving me though I kick hard against it, racing in the dark against spectral Seine-by-late-late boatloads of tourists.

"*Cyn-thheee-ahh,*" I yell, voice echoing against the bridge's pitch underside.

I duck under, kicking hard with my legs, feeling my sneakers heavy, angling for the bank, remembering in a strange vivid flash a fat sunburned lifeguard in a rowboat yelling directions. Midlake, we take off our blue jeans, blow them into an inflatable vest. I stroke for what looks like a stairwell.

When I pull up onto the slanting stone embankment beyond

the stairs, breathless and cold, I look back at the water. Cynthia's angling toward me, feet splashing behind, arms stroking a tight crawl. Above on the quay several people yell and point. Cynthia pulls up beside me, grinning and gasping, wiping drops of water from her forehead.

"Look," I ask, eyeing her like I'm a specialist. "Are you mad?"

She rolls her eyes, raises her forearm to her face, scrunches her nose, starting to laugh, her hands spreading to suggest, *entre nous, maybe I am*, her head arching back.

"I can't believe you did that. We'll glow in the dark," I say, still trying to catch my breath, calm myself from the thrill of smashing against water.

"Was that the dog paddle?" Cynthia asks, laughing so hard while she tries to catch her breath that she coughs.

Opals of light glisten from the ends of her hair. She coughs again and I slap her back a few times. A light wind blows over us, clothes clinging to our skin.


My sack is mercifully still on the ledge; the wind on the bridge chills. I put on a sweater and hand Cynthia a sweatshirt. We walk toward her hotel along the Boulevard St. Germain. From across the street, I scan the front tables of the Café Cluny, but don't see Stunts and Surface. It's drizzling slightly and we walk arm in arm, elegantly sopping. We pass a small Italian man and I overhear him say to an English girl, "Turn, I have something for you to look at," and when she turns I follow her glance to a striped umbrella that she must have forgotten, now mounted and opened atop a Mercedes, spread like a sunflower to the street lights. She cocks her head coyly, clasps her hands in mock delight, and I'm steeped in that jealousy we feel at another's resourceful, well-timed touch.

Standing in the mouth of Cynthia's hotel she pulls me toward her and puts her arms around me and we kiss, her tongue tickling my palate. When we break I tell her I'd planned on ringing Yvonne to see about crashing at her place. If Yvonne and Quinn are there we can all go out to dinner. If they're not, the two of us can go for dinner and wine. Cynthia kisses me again, as if she hasn't heard me and the suggestion is sheer evasiveness, or stupidity, and this time I put my arms around her, wondering, half-hopefully, whether something has clicked. A group of Australians makes gestures behind us. Four of them, puckering their lips, miming embraces, fingers massaging their own shoulders. Cynthia's really kissing now, her eyes pressed shut.

"Jesus H. Christ, mate," one drawls. "Get a room."

"Just ignore the kangaroo court," Cynthia whispers.

## 11

Quinn's place looks out over slate rooftops, a roofscape composed of slants and jumbled geometric forms, tiles glistening like fish scales in the bright morning sun, wall pipes, chimneys, antennae jutting, patterns of shingles all slants and planes receding to the Eiffel Tower in the distance.

"Quinn's?" Cynthia asks of the sketches.

"Ummmmm. . . . Yeah."

"They're spare; he's really a purist," Cynthia says.

"Oh, you're right," Yvonne says, going to the kitchen. "He'll never grow up."

"Look, there's Jason," Cynthia says. "Next to an ape."

"Hello," Quinn says, opening the door, a wicker shopping basket in hand, a bright-red choker around his neck. "Hello you too," he says, bowing to the orangutan, aping its bizarre gesture, making a face. "My God, there were some stupid Americans at the market, unbelievable."

"How are you feeling, Quinn?" I ask.

"The usual aches and pains," he says, coughing deeply, and then, raising his hand. "Oh, that's nothing."

"Anyone want coffee?" Yvonne calls over the roar of her hair dryer. She's drying her hair in front of a toaster, reading a book of Op Art.

"I like using a toaster as a mirror," she says. "Anything I don't like I can blame on the distortions."

"Coffee would be great," Cynthia says.

We settle into a brunch of croissants, brioches, pâté de foie gras, Camembert and *vin de pays*, stripping off strands of the buttery, warm bread.

"Have some pâté," Quinn says to Yvonne.

"Did your tongue touch that fork?" Yvonne asks.

"What's wrong with his tongue?" Cynthia asks.

"It's green," I say.

"His palate's jaded," Yvonne says. "Quinn has a list of ailments as long as *Paradise Lost*."

"Paradise. You'll see," Quinn says. "Lost. I'll have my autopsy reports mailed to the whole pack of you."

"Do you really think American tourists are worse than any others?" Cynthia asks.

"Yes," Quinn says. "They are the worst. Absolutely. Not all of them, but most of them."

"Calm down now, Quinn," Yvonne says. "Cynthia, please. You'll activate one of his conditions."

"What's so bad about Americans?" Cynthia asks, playing to Quinn.

Quinn twists off a piece of croissant and spreads butter and then pâté over it. He eats with a tremendous show of animation, though little food actually passes into his mouth, like his mind is half on his food and half on the subject.

"To Amerotrash," Quinn says, "Europe is like a cultural Parcourse Fitness Circuit."

"But what about the Germans?" I ask. "In a Portuguese café I saw a German scrape his full plate to his poodle in front of the restaurant owner."

"Yes, the Germans are bad," Quinn says. "The best are ostentatiously guilty."

"And the worst?" Cynthia asks.

"They're like Americans."

"What about the Japanese?" Cynthia asks.

"The Japanese," Quinn says, "are like . . . like . . . aliens. They look surprised by everything."

"Why don't you tell us about Canadians?" Yvonne says.

Quinn spreads his hands.

"Jason?" Yvonne asks.

"He's right," I say. "Canotrash are just too Swiss for words."


At night we go to *The One-Armed Swimmer.* The backdrop is at first Vegas, *Sands* and *Caesar's* in neon script, Duesenberg magenta, white-walled, all the main characters in casino regalia, low-cut red cocktail uniforms, gamblers in glitzy sports coats, gold chains, oversize rings, glow-in-the-dark earrings, much dancing in the center of the revolving stages, painted with the red/black/green stripes and numbers of a roulette wheel that turns like the plot around the cat-and-mouse game between a torch singer in scanty dress and a slick gambler in love with a cocktail waitress. Pure desire carried out at frantic pace, characters ducking in and out of the shafts of greens and reds, cardboard rainbows descending over slot machines, scene gradually shifting so that it is now not Nevada but something tropical, Bali or Bora Bora, thatched bars and Japanese parasols in mai tais, a slow-motion strangling in strobe light, the stage and wheel of lights moving in circles, like the one-armed swimmer?

Stunts stands rigidly in the back of the orchestra between two other slide trombonists, crook over his shoulder, slightly angled, the embouchure forcing his face into a grimacing smile, arm moving back and forward in power rhythms, the three trombones ducking from side to side in marching-band sync, the loud, redundant sequences so enmeshed with other sounds it's hard to get the phrasing. The guy to his left's got on one of those Nazi U-boat hats dishwashers or guitar gods wear.

Surface sits to the side of the horns in a row of three drummers, in a Hawaiian shirt splashed with color, his head ringed with a gold sweatband, a long carnation tucked behind it. I try to follow the quick moments of calypso swing from drum to drum, to connect motion to sound. When I don't concentrate it seems like noise, mere banging and none of that leaving out of small things that accentuates what's left in. And even when I think I've got the beat I'm not sure it isn't pounding. The hands move too fast to be precise—flashing, violent, chopping, then graceful, like time-delayed opening of flowers, as if the drums rise to his hands, hands up and down like he's tracing patterns in the air, palms cupped in freeze frames and then accelerating down, sweat pouring over his gleaming face.

We've been sitting around a table in front of the Café Cluny for an hour after the show, drinking a fine Margaux, the evening languid, none of us disposed to speak. The air is warm and full of sounds and I feel myself drifting. When a woman at the next table jiggles the ice in her glass the sound reaches me like dice over a backgammon board from a distant room. The shuffle and patter of human traffic and street noises come momentarily together with the ooze and drip and sass of jazz. People stride by, dresses rustle, a distant car horn flugles, shoes click on the pavement, someone screeches two tables together, a vaguely familiar cream-colored Cadillac pulls up. Passengers spill out, one-two-three-four-five; the car honks, once, twice, its hood drawn up, a slide-trombone pumping out the front passenger window, and then the car peels out.

"Emma and Angélique of Paris," Surface says, straightening his suit, then introducing the girls to Yvonne, Cynthia, and Quinn with a bow. "And Marcy of the French suburb of Houston."

"You dance in the line," Quinn says.

"What sharp little eyes you have," Marcy says.

Cynthia's face has a healthy, vibrant quality as she shakes with the girls; she eyes Stunts with amusement and strains to understand Angélique and Emma when they slide into French. When she tries to answer in French, Emma corrects her with lazy precision. Emma has an unnaturally small nose; her face is olive, her hair black and short. I don't follow their words, but watch how Emma's fingers flutter and her nose squinches when she corrects Cynthia, and how Cynthia encourages the corrections and then bends her ear forward to get the sound, nods her head, repeats what she's heard.

Quinn, who has been reserved for the past hour, takes a sketch pad out of his pocket and asks Stunts if he minds. Stunts sits erect, profiling with his jaw thrust forward, and the head takes shape, gains features, shading, then two dark pupils.

"Damn," Stunts says when Quinn's done, grabbing the pad off the table. "Do you mind?"

The pad in front of him, he whips out his knife and cuts precisely around the drawing.

"Now I feel like I've really been to France," Stunts says, dripping wine on the cut-out of his face.

Quinn, who has watched Stunts stolidly, retrieves the defaced pad. Where Stunts's head was there is now a bowl of fruit from the drawing underneath, making the sheet look like a painted silhouette. Quinn studies the head-shaped fruits, sips his wine, and toasts Stunts, a deep irony in his face.

Several blonde Americans pass, leaving an after-image of their backs bent by the sort of mammoth Jansport packs one might use for an extended polar expedition.

"Where on earth do you think they're going like that?" I hear Marcy asking, and Surface is answering, "Rue de Nepal."

Stunts looks down at the cut-out drawing of his head again, then tucks it into the pocket of his camouflage shirt. Next thing, chair kicked out behind him, crossing the street, he weaves through cars as if on a military errand under fire.

"Alors, pourquoi so much blue in your face?" Emma asks me, carrying her chair next to mine and throwing one leg over my thigh.

I can't think what to say. Cynthia is talking with Yvonne. I catch a few words about the shape of the architecture, lines of the boulevards, and the pink and blue tints of the streets.

Emma shrugs at me; she's wearing the chic where's-the-flood jeans that were a symbol of nerddom in junior high, and one of those striped French sailor T-shirts I've always coveted and plan on stockpiling. I don't move her leg off me.

"The buildings do seem a little blue," I say, filling her wine glass.

"It is the air that is blue, silly," she whispers in my ear. "Not the buildings."

When Stunts returns, he sets a blood-soaked bag on the table, and gestures the waiter over.

"Garçon," he says, opening the bag to reveal a steak. "Do you think you might heat this up?"

"Ce n'est pas possible," the waiter says. And offers to bring a menu or recommend for us a good place for dining.

Stunts sits staring at the meat, like a denied dog.

"Dommage," Angélique says.

"Tartare then," Stunts says, and produces the knife and addresses the meat, carving off a few rubbery chunks, then slicing them into strips.

"Ça c'est trop tartare pour moi," Angélique says.

Stunts picks up a strip between index finger and thumb, bites off a piece, and puts the remnant down, daubing his lips with his napkin.

"Rather on the chewy side," he says. "But it has taste."

Stunts hands Marcy a slice, and she bites off half of it, making a noisy, smacking sound; a little blood runs out of the side of her mouth. She hands me the other half of the slice and I shrug and pop it in my mouth. The meat tastes a bit like blood-flavored bubble gum. I finish my wine and pour myself another glass, wave off the next offered slice, pat my stomach like I'm full.

Yvonne and Quinn get up.

"Lovely friends you make, Jason," Yvonne says to me, imitating a British accent.

"Rather," I say.

Stunts looks from her to me, amused. "Not staying for dinner?" he asks.

"Regrettably, we have already eaten," Quinn says.

"I think I'll go too," Cynthia says, getting up and putting her string purse over her shoulder.

Feeling me straighten, Emma swings her leg off mine. I want to tell Cynthia to sit down, have a drink, relax, loosen up, even if I don't want to relax and would rather be doing something else, if I could figure out something worth doing.

"You okay?" I ask Cynthia, bothered by the scene, and my own unprovoked recoil.

"Of course I'm okay," she says, dusting off her jeans.

"You don't want to sit a few minutes?" I say.

"Jason, I'll see you," she says, forcing a smile.

Watching her back, I think I shouldn't let her go, that she's slipping from me in a visible way, like tired fingers letting go, slipping through lack of energy. I should run after her, slip my arm through hers, maybe go for a walk around the gardens; we could scale a fence and wade in a fountain, that's a thought. No question, I should go after her. But right now, feeling pressured, I would rather stay seated than anything else. Minutes pass. Maybe I could take another route and surprise her in front of the hotel. But maybe that would not be such a great surprise.

Stunts holds a strip of meat out to Emma, who opens her mouth and lets him place it on her tongue. She keeps stroking her hair, fingers running through it like a comb. When not in her hair her hands smooth the collar of her open leather jacket, as if she's reminding herself she's got on a leather jacket. She puts her leg over mine again, jeans sliding up to reveal patterned leather boots, and I put my hand on her leg, and we look at each other, and I think how some women just know when you're supposed to be taken, how available you are, how they can play with that. With that thought I toast glasses with her, and then she puts her glass down and pecks me on the cheek, leaning up against me so I can feel that she's not wearing a bra, her shoulder and stomach pressing against mine, and when I finally peck her cheek back she laughs, shakes her hair, exposes some neck. I lick her neck and growl. Stunts punches me on the arm and gives me thumbs up. Emma shoots him the finger.

The table has become a mess, strips of meat lying next to corks and bloodied napkins. Two elderly tourists at the next table settle their checks and depart. Stunts sees an enormous lady with a feathered hat and a poodle and goes over and gives the little dog a piece that it lip-lickingly eats.

"There's enough room in those britches for both of us," Stunts says to me, leaning over Emma.

Our soirée is interrupted by the manager and a burly man carrying an empty wine bottle, his shirt a pastiche of smears.

"A man with a bottle can't be all bad," Surface says, squinting at the man.

"Veuillez quitter cette table immédiatement," the manager

says, and insists that if we do not leave, he will telephoné the police.

"Come on," Marcy says, sliding Surface a napkin on which she's penned a multiplication sign and a question mark.

"Anytime," Surface says, wiping his lips with the napkin.

"Until you can't stand it. Tell that waiter his cologne smells like a condom."

"Messieurs!"

"Let's split," Surface says. "I don't want to spend the night kicking the shit out of frogs."


It's a long walk back to the hotel through winding streets. A man walks by with a bulbous plastered splint on his middle finger as if he's misread directions in a sex shop. Halfway to the hotel, I stop in a disco/bar for a nightcap. The bartender hands me a scotch and soda before I order, somebody's mistake. I watch the couples dancing, not seeing many places I'd like to cut in. One man dances alone with almost no movement, disdain on his face. He makes slight flicks of his feet like he's shaking shit off his shoes. A statuesque white man, head shaven, spins a tiny, solid black man in a wild hustle, gyrating him, allowing him to stay on axis without spinning out of control because he keeps going faster, suddenly, incomprehensibly, changing directions, until all moments but the freeze of direction-change are a blur.


Cynthia's reading Kundera's *The Unbearable Lightness of Being*, wearing her Smith sweatshirt, hair done up in a bun, a few frizzy hairs out. When I sit on her bed, she sets the book down. I know I should apologize for how I acted, try to explain it, but I'm feeling dizzy and hot, removed from her moodiness. She doesn't say anything, waiting for me to speak, then reaching for her book.

"I'm sorry," I manage.

"What for?"

"For being messed up," I say.

"Sorry for being drunk?"

"No," I say. "I didn't mean that."

"Aren't you flattering yourself just a little?"

The phrase, a Julie staple, brings blood into my face. The last thing drunk people want is a scene involving a critique of the skewed and inflated nature of their self-perception with a sober person.

"I'm sorry for acting like . . . Calabacillas."

"Who?"

"In the paint—"

"Jason. Why didn't you just go off with that French Custard Dish?" she says.

"Which one?"

"You know which one . . . God, the air is so blue. You were practically drooling."

I start to say *Emma seemed more like a chocolate mousse than a custard, though I haven't tasted her,* but catch myself.

"I didn't want to go off with her," I say, but I can't quite bring myself to say, *I want to be with you,* though right now it would be true enough.

"You know, Jason," she says, voice calm, distressingly sincere, like she's more sorry for me than angry, "there's something missing in you. It's like you really want to be involved with somebody but you just can't. You acted like I wasn't there."

I unlace my shoes, unbutton my shirt, look blankly at my shoes.

"It's like you're waiting for someone to be Julie again, and you just don't want to be by yourself."

"I've been by myself for six months," I say, stretching out behind her. She's still sitting up.

"Six months. What an achievement. Tell me, if she knocked on that door right now . . ."

"The Custard?"

"Julie."

She's looking at me like there is a midmorning talk-show caption saying "obsessed lover" under my face.

"Julie?" I say, and shake my head in protest.

"If she knocked on the door right now and said . . ."

"What are you talking about Julie for? She's not about to knock on any door."

"That's not the point."

"Look," I say. "That's *finito*."

"When people use foreign words at the ends of sentences they're usually finessing something."

"Let's get this straight," I say. "If room service wheeled Julie in on a fur-lined platter with caviar in her navel, a bottle of Napoleon brandy in one hand and a jar of Vaseline in the other, I'd send her back to the kitchen with my compliments."

"Even in denial you're fantasizing," she says.

I look at her, the frizzy curls, the implied curve of waist under the sweatshirt and I move toward her, backhand the book off the bed. Her lower lip protruding, shaking her head slightly, she lets me turn her around and sit behind her and massage her neck.

"Do you think people can change?" I ask. "Or do they just think they're changing when it's obvious to any outsider they're just making variations of the same mistakes?"

"I think if people really want to change they can change," she says, turning and looking at me with a tickled, searching expression that makes me feel emotionally delinquent.

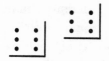

# 12

When you've been evasive in patching things you can see the patches, all the stitched evasions. A relationship only exists at the level of the least committed person, Fred says.

Cynthia's sleeping beside me, but I can't sleep. A hard reddish light slants through the window, glowing on the foot of the bed, on Cynthia's feet intertwined with sheets. The light hums. When I touch Cynthia's face she moves slightly, wincing like a mosquito has landed on her. It feels like we've argued, that I've pushed her to argue, that all along she's been straighter with me than I've been with her, that I could never achieve her plane of openness. This disturbs at both ends. The memory of our silences, of the frayed conversation, the edge in her tone make the silence of the room feel like déjà vu.

"Don't be so innocent," Julie says.

"I'm not innocent."

"Of course you are."

"I'm not innocent, Julie. I really don't think I am."

"Then how are you wrong?"

"I don't know," I say, and, aha, I'm gutter-snagged.

At first those arguments were sportive, competitive, a form of foreplay. In the dark I could always hear Julie scratch her neck and swallow, the small click in her throat indicating she was readying herself to speak about something that upset her, something that, if sensitive, I should ask about before she could bring up the subject, that *she* always had to bring subjects up. We argued more and more about not communicating, which never made sense to me, because she wanted me to agree that we couldn't agree. Even then, in those arguments that were never about whatever they were about—that were probably as much about my *frittering away potential* as about anything else—I always found something charming in her oddly effective illogic. But in the end she was right in her way, just as now, lying here unable or unwilling to make myself stop thinking about arguments with Julie, Cynthia is right.

The time we really fought Julie was certainly right, though it appears she was already seeing Hallmark. They went to dinner and the movies a few times when I was working. I couldn't believe she'd be seriously interested in anyone so rectangular. After the fight, chastened, I crawled back. We had two decent weeks, went to Fire Island for a weekend, some *marshmallows flambeaux*, her phrase. But now it's clear we were done; she had weighed her options, taken stock, and decided. Maybe that's just as well.

I looked haggard when I got back from the casino that night. I hadn't slept or shaved in two days, since cutting out after acid words in a restaurant. She looked at me and got a whiff of the casino and did not like what she smelled. I was exhausted in a way other than tiredness. I'd won three hundred. But it had been a disastrous night. It's hard to explain. Sometimes in gambling it's better not to have won a lot and then lost most of it than to have lost straight off.

When you've been up real cash in a casino and known that

you should quit—use a small fork on a big lobster—and wondered even as you watched the blackjack shoe that was rearing to kick you, wondered why it is characteristic of the species not to walk out of casinos at the right time, then you feel, with the sense of permanent damage that attends every failure, that the night's been disastrous, and even as you hope that the night's slide into loss may not matter in the long run, somehow you know you'll remember it, and you do.

I'd been up seven thousand dollars after three hours and had gone and eaten the three-pound lobster with drawn butter, put on the illustrated bib and all the while known I should go home, patch things up with Julie. Quit all the backgammon. Quit the late shifts. With that casino cash we could go on a trip. I could bow and scrape with tickets to Paris or Portugal in my hand. We could move to a bigger place and get some furniture.

But I stayed in the casino two and a half days.

And on the two-hour bus ride back I felt with cool surety and futility how pathetic the nights had been. I could see the whole run into exhaustion, to the point way past where it was all just chips, and I was letting a month's rent ride on a roll, not caring if I won or lost, wanting only to get out of the place for a whiff of air but unable to leave, all of it distant next to the sense that Julie, whom I was pissing off, was the best thing, the only real thing in my life. And yet when I closed my eyes all I could see were the colors and edges of the dice and cards, sequences lucid, every combination spinning two-by-two into the ark, dice dancing, showing this face and that. Pair of aces, ace-ace. Crap out. Dice to the same shooter. Pair of sixes, box cars, crap again, pay twelve. Dice to the same shooter, shake those dice, sir. Luck to you, shooter. Four-four, pay hard eight. Place the odds on the eight.

I let myself in quietly, feeling the remorseful truant's longing for understanding or at least a light sentence, walking doggishly with my tail between my legs, hoping she'd see how much it had hurt me to act as I had, that it had hurt me as much as it hurt her—but, well, one way or the other, that's not true. All might be well.

She was dozing in front of a western, but when the door clicked open she burst awake and started raving, flushed, livid, venomous, screaming in my face. I'd bought a rose from a religious zombie in the bus station and she snatched the by-now sickly flower and crumpled it and then stamped on it.

"You should be ashamed to come back here. I don't want that sad flower. I don't want to talk to you."

"I am ashamed," I say.

"Gambler!"

"No more. . . . You're all the excitement I need. More."

After the smoke of the casino and then the refrigerated bus ride, my voice ekes out.

"Don't try to pacify me," Julie screams. Her foot is still on the rose. She sees it there and squashes it more. "You're not going to pacify me. You compulsive . . . you . . . gambler."

"I'm not a compulsive . . . ," I say.

"You are, you're compulsive."

"Julie, be reasonable."

"Be reasonable. You tell me to be reasonable. You stay away for two days and you tell me to be reasonable. I am reasonable. You can just take a. . . . You're not reasonable. You should get help. Not compulsive. Not compulsive. You should go to, what's it called . . ."

"Please," I say. "I tried to call . . ."

"You tried!" she shrieks, the veins perilously full and dancing on her neck. And it's really a shriek, a sound I've never heard out of her mouth. "Tell that story to a shrink. I don't want to hear it. Never again. No more *yuppie slime* for you, never ever ever."

"I didn't mean that. I tried . . ."

"Oh, thank you for taking time off from your gambling. I can imagine how hard that was for you. You tore yourself from the table just to talk to me, or did you have a waitress bring you a cellular phone? Was I supposed to be waiting up all night by the phone? If you must know, I took that phone off the hook, you bastard."

"Julie," I say. "I'm tired. You can hear that I can barely talk. I'm sorry. I'm really sorry. I really am. What can I say? Can you turn that TV off?"

"No!"

"Then change the channel."

"Don't . . ."

"There's enough cowboys and Indians in here," I say, suddenly laughing awkwardly.

"Don't . . ."

"Come on, Fruit Slice."

"Don't you dare try funniness or any of that Fruit Slice business."

"Have you been drinking?"

"No, I haven't!" she yells.

"I can smell it on you. You shouldn't drink. It's late. We should get some sleep."

"You mean I should calm down, that I'm overreacting. That we can go to bed and it'll be okay in the morning. Yes, I've been drinking! Give me one good reason why I shouldn't be drinking!"

"Julie, you get delirious when you drink. You rave at flower pots."

"You should be in a flower pot," she shrieks. "You'd probably grow."

I've never seen her so mad. Nearly crazy. And I've made her this way. There's a perverse momentary vanity in knowing this that's overwhelmed by the sense that she's right and there really isn't anything to say, that she shouldn't forgive me easily, maybe ever, that you can't just take it back, that mistakes are mistakes and go on forever. My head throbs with exhaustion.

"Julie," I say. "I really love you. We all make mistakes."

"You mean, let he who is without sin cast the first . . . dice. That's what you mean. Cast the first dice, cast the dice, dice, *dice*," she yells, laughing in a strained way through her anger, like she's landed a stored-up punch line that hurts her with its accuracy.

"I thought we weren't going to be funny," I say, my voice gravelly as a loan shark's.

"Jason. Get out of here," she says. "Just slime out of here, you slime. I can't stand the sight of you. Checkmate, you bastard."

"Checkmate," I say, nodding, pressing my lips shut. "Can't stand the slime of me, checkmate, okay, *okay*."

Feeling too exhausted to argue, I walk right out into Riverside Park and sit under an elm and start thinking over the last three days, trying to follow a switchbacking trail of events to some clearing where I was innocent.

We argued in that restaurant. I commented on the busboy's silverware-work and she said *you sure oughta know*. We exchanged a quick flurry, and before I knew it she was storming out, leaving nine-dollars and ninety-five cents worth of a nineteen-dollar Alaska King Crab on her plate. I sat in the restaurant feeling numb and pissed at her and ate the untouched second leg. When the waitress asked whether everything was okay I told her my wife had just gone home with food poisoning but that the chef shouldn't take it personally, and I sat there, in spite of myself remembering how the first time we ate in that restaurant Julie, as ever delighted by the specialness of cracking an unfamiliar menu in a promising seafood restaurant, "ooohed" and "aaahed," performing down the menu, moaning about how starved she was and then just nibbling away at each giant Thai shrimp. A thing of hers. Then when we get home she attacks leftovers with a fork in each hand.

When I got home she called me *a case of downward mobility* and refused to talk. I yelled at her, said she was getting like her *yuppie slime friends*, cracked some joke about a *yuppie's favorite whine*. She didn't say another word, just put her hands over her ears, cowered and cringed like I was liable to hit her. Then I stuffed some waiter cash in my pocket and got on a bus. Impulse move. Or was it? Then the win streak. And all the time that sense of cowardice, running, deferring, perversely missing the point.

Bugs play about my head. The whole place itches. I wonder if I'm really compulsive.

Am I?

Certainly not a pure addict like old Slav—Slav the magnificent—who, mirthful even in defeat, puts action before eating and sleeping, who owes everybody he's ever met money but chirps continuously. Slav's life is all gambling.

"I no here," he says, if his wife calls.

"Where are you?" Pincus the Houseman yells, his hand over the phone.

"I go in the movies," Slav yells, and turns alarmingly purple with laughter.

"He hasn't been here all day," Pincus says into the receiver.

Sometimes Slav's wife sits at the table behind the game, a kerchief done up a face so large and excessively blank it looks like she's been shocked too many times.

Certainly I'm not compulsive like Sammy, who's so haunted by the theory of games he's bored by playing them, and plays only occasionally for survival expenses, because, unfortunately, theoreticians have to eat. Not compulsive like Acer, that cynical addict to whom everything's just a game within a game, a game one can't help playing, though one is condemned to suffer play against cretins.

Mostly I spend an hour or two before work. And every week or two I hit Atlantis with some friends from the restaurant. You think you shouldn't go, but you want to, so you do. You think how you'll get off the bus and they will give you twelve dollars in quarters and tickets for the all-you-can-eat buffet. Good food. Drinks on the house. All of this is nice. Where's the compulsion?

But the scary thought comes to me that lately I have been weird and absurd, impatient with everything, hardly able to stand people's chatter. Maybe I've been this way for a long time. Or all along. Though I think of myself as a person of above-average sanity, say, seven or eight on a scale of ten, I actually might need to wear a straight jacket on formal occasions. Why, for instance, am I not steeped in remorse, genuinely contrite? Why do I just sit here thinking, *Yes I'm badly in the wrong and must change my act but there's nothing to be done about it right now and I basically mean well and with love there's got to be a deeper understanding?* So that nothing, not even Julie's forgiveness, matters as much right now as a major breakfast, a steaming shower, the cool sleekness of sheets.

A squirrel darts across my line of vision, looks furtively in both directions, cuts out. I've passed right through the tiredness to the point of hazy calmness, and none of it touches me anymore. Those were other people yelling back in our crowded little room. I'm sitting by the Hudson River with three hundred dollars I won in a casino. I'll watch the sunrise. And when the sunrise ends I'll walk across town for forty-dollar custom scrambled eggs, sausage, a large fresh-squeezed juice at the Four Seasons, if they'll let me in the door.

DICE AGAIN

# 13

A raucous trombone solo bottoms out, rounds a tight corner, and is just groan-sliding into a coasting section when, wrapped in a bedspread, I jerk open the hotel door.

Stunts lowers the trombone, as if interrupted, shows his teeth, settles the bell and slide back into a Yamaha case Angélique's holding out, and then snaps the case shut. Surface has one arm around Marcy, the other around Emma. Both of the girls have large wicker beach bags over their shoulders. Several chaotic heads of hair, disgruntled faces over bathrobes, lean out of rooms.

Cynthia has propped herself against the bedstead, wrapped in a sheet, rubbing sleep out of her eyes.

"Sorry to barge in on your toga party," Stunts says.

"We thought we'd invite y'all on an expedition that begins about ten minutes from now," Surface says. "'Course, if you gone and booked another engagement . . ."

I look at Cynthia blankly.

"Where to?" Cynthia asks Marcy, turning from me.

"What's the difference?" Marcy says.

Cynthia lets the sheet slide and reaches slowly for her sweatshirt.

Stunts whistles.

"Yousa, yousa," Surface says.

"Just get dressed," Cynthia says to me.


Hours later, Cynthia's reddish hair streams back in the wind; she looks over her shoulder as if to say something, then throws up her hands to gather her hair. Her mirrored sunglasses, borrowed from Surface, reflect our passage through braided grapefields, acres of future Alsace. I picture farmers' daughters purple to midthigh in wood tuns, purple-stained lips. All of them named Fifi. In the tun, the nouveau, Fifi, really, Fifi darling—oh for a swig of such vintage—this will make for a good year all around.

We pass inn after inn announcing *English Spoken Here*, and when the sun's blazing directly overhead Marcy stops at a quaint ivy-covered inn that announces *English Spoken Here* on a placard in the window. Surface takes an enormous, polyurethane chest cooler from the trunk. Cynthia and I lean against the cream Cadillac. Marcy's breasts swell a zebra-striped leotard; her hair rises in a coiled braid like a blond anaconda.

"Like I say, you invited to a party," Surface says, lifting the cooler onto the hood.

"When's this party start already?" Marcy says.

Surface opens the cooler and takes out several bottles of cold white wine.

"Wrong, girl," he says. "When do it end?"


Stunts assumes the wheel and the car speeds, flirts with the curves, plays with the road. I lie my head on Cynthia's shoulder in the front seat, looking up, and the cloudscapes wash by. We bank through rows of poplars, straightening upon Germany at accelerated speeds, waved through by bored customs officers, then passing back and forth chilled, full-bodied Alsace until, with the sun blood orange but still high over wind-heaving fields of marigold and wheat, Stunts spots a small isolated siloed farm and yells *whoa boy*, easing the car, *easy boy, easy.* We park about a kilometer away from the farm. Stunts opens the dashboard and draws out a .38 special. He snaps open the gun and chambers six rounds. There's an apple core on the car floor and he pockets it.

"Now, about that barbecue," Stunts says.

"What's the apple for?" Marcy asks.

"Let's go," Stunts says.

"Right, Jason?" Surface says, peeling off his jacket and tie and rolling up the sleeves of a shiny blue shirt with a Satin American label.

Cynthia frowns at the gun and lies back, draping her hair over the seat. I pommel-horse out of the car.

"Gonna get us a pig," Stunts whispers when we are on our bellies, elbowing arm over arm over jimson and clover, the Elmer's latex gunk of stray crushed milkweeds sticky on my arms, creeping up on a pigpen outdoors in a wood shed apart from the main.

"That apple for the pig's mouth?" I whisper.

"Naw," Surface says.

The animals squeal at our approach. And suddenly I'm remembering the blood rush of sticking up that Mexican before the apartment sale.

A woman screamed across the Holiday Bar. "You're hurting me, asshole, it isn't funny anymore."

"Hey," I intervened. Fred, who'd joined me for a nightcap, tried to sit me back down by grabbing my coat. The Mexican was slapping the woman; she had a handful of his hair.

"Hey," I yelled into the screaming, heart pounding. I came

at him with my hand under my jacket, almost convinced I had a gun. "Make your play or get out of Dodge."

"Dodge?"

"Make your play, amigo. Draw poker or scram."

He narrowed his eyes, the two of us squinting and counter-squinting until I thumbed my nose at him, fingers of my free hand wiggling.

"Come on, Johnny, honey," the woman said, stroking her husband's neck, voice syrupy between bloodied lips. "Let's go somewhere decent where there ain't no freaking maniacs and have us a drink."

Fred accompanied me out of the bar, gripping me in a stumbling bear hug.

"Hey, wait," he kept saying. "Jason, man, wait. You packing a piece?"

"Get off me, Fred," I said.

"Jason," he said, laugh strained. "Let it all run off you, man. I'll get you an alibi. Meantime, get some reflector glasses and wear them backwards. Get some 3-D glasses. And stop jostling me, man. Just take it easy."

I was struggling to get loose but he wouldn't let go, kept rocking me back and forth, squeezing the breath out of me.

"Get it together," he said. "Don't be so hostile, man. So your girlfriend fired you. So she's someone else's girlfriend. So you don't have to go sticking people up."

"Seriously, man," I said. "Let go of me."

And when he did I side-kicked the menu box off a restaurant. The next day, ashamed, I would see the manager's moron son hammering the box back into place.

Stunts moves upon the pen where the pigs circle in the muck, undersides spattered, coming for him when he shows the apple, rushing for feed, dirty, comical, flat-nosed. Surface eases open the pen, bracing with his forearm while Stunts holds forth the apple and the pigs squeeze upon the gate until a little one manages through and darts with a squeal into the field—and they say a pig has a higher IQ than a dog—small and swift, parting the grass startlingly fast, then moving slower, head poking about as if suddenly realizing it's lost and, worse, endangered, while we fan out, trotting after with hunched backs barely visible and steering it away from the farm until we are far into the field and Stunts draws the revolver and steadies it over his arm—there's a report—and hits the pig in the hind so that it staggers, amazed, frantic, and Stunts runs at it pumping several rounds behind its ear while it rolls and jerks in clonic spasms, vibrating, frenzied, spewing.

Surface and I watch the farm, glancing now at the writhing creature, now at the surprisingly still farm and granary, a silo from which I expect, momentarily, farmers riding Clydesdales and clothed like Pennsylvania Quakers to come running with pitchforks.

The pig's eyes roll crazily. When it is still, Surface scoops up the bloody baggage, blood staining his shirt as we trot toward the car, Stunts opening the trunk and Surface heaving in the pig, stripping open his bloody shirt to bare a massive chest dark and dazzled with sweat.

Stunts floors the wide empty highways, brakes finally onto smaller roads, and a dirt road off across fields to a small pear-shaped pond, fringed by light-leaved aspens and white poplars; there's a clearing, half muck-filled, and green water against swaying trees and a field of green wheat. The sun's just above the fields, bathing the landscape in orange light.

Stunts takes the pig by its hind legs and carries it down by the water, where Surface and he start washing it, and when the pig is clean they carry it over to the ice-filled cooler and dump it in with the sodas and wine.

"Come on, girls," Marcy says, stripping off her skirt and leotard and splashing into the pond. "Who's got shampoo?"

I sit on a mossy rock by the bank with Cynthia. We watch the girls soap one another, lather their hair, laugh and splash, dunk one another. Bubbles spread in clusters around them on the pond. Cynthia's been in a quiet mood since seeing the bloodied pig and sits with the tail end of a grass stalk in her mouth.

"Les Grandes Baigneuses," she says.

"Three Women Bathers, you mean," I say.

"Do you think those pig killers are safe?"

"They're safe."

"They seem just slightly above on-all-fours on the evolutionary scale," she says.

"They're okay. But any time you want to hit the road . . ."

"We'll just steal a couple of horses."


Campfire flames glow orange. It's night. We pass a bottle of wine, conjugating the German verb *drinken, drunk, gedrunken.* Stunts goes to the car trunk and takes out a trash bag full of tapes and claps country music into a ghetto blaster. Immediately the French girls are rising, arms locking shoulders in a Rockettes line, doing a hybrid cancan western hustle while Surface drums along the edge of the cooler with two char-halved sticks, his hands blurs of shape, his shoulders swiveling.

"Come powder your little French noses," Surface yells. "Toot those tight little coke-ette horns."

"Qu'est-ce que tu dis?"

"Toot-ez vous, cocaine," Marcy says.

"Comment dit-on *do a line of cocaine* en français?" Cynthia asks Emma, who's just sniffed a line.

"Prendre de la cocaïne?"

"Excellent," I say. "There a soda in there?"

Stunts lifts one of the pig's feet out of the cooler, then lets it drop and tosses me a Diet Pepsi. The pop-ring crunches inward with a hiss-snap; I suck down the froth. Mirror circles, lines through a rolled bill. Cynthia hesitates, then passes the mirror.

"Girl, you ever try coke?" Marcy asks Cynthia.

"A few times," Cynthia says, nodding, seeming a little slowed on the uptake by the wine.

"How about Pepsi?" Stunts asks.

"Cynthia," I say, suddenly gesturing at the can. "Did you realize Pepsi Cola's an anagram for episcopal?"

"Share a line with me," Marcy says to Cynthia.

"Don't if you don't want to," I say.

"What do you mean by that?"

I snort my lines like a fiend, sealing one nostril, then the other with pond water; against the disappearing sense of my teeth, the Pepsi has a narcotic fizzle: soda poppy.

"If only we had buffaloed eggs," Marcy says, snuffling.

"What are they?" Cynthia asks.

"I don't know," Marcy says. "But they must exist."

"Yeah," I say. "And if you see an albino deer, Krazy-glue a horn on its head."

"Miss Cynthia, have a line," Surface says. "You'll like it. Powder your virgin nose. Buffalo gal, come out tonight."

"Don't if you don't want to," I say again—numbly—the first comets projecting across the planetary dome in my skull.

"You maybe like this," Emma says, licking her teeth.

"Don't listen to her," I say, following some mean impulse to press up against her reluctance.

"What the hell," Cynthia says.

"Right," Stunts says. "What the fuck."

"Pardon his French," Surface says.

"Are you positive?" Stunts says, peering at her with mock seriousness.

"Oh, cook off," Cynthia says, glowers. He smiles his I-put-razors-in-kids'-Halloween-apples smile.

Some mosquito activity has begun; I smudge one on my cheek.

"Surface, man. Roll us a number to keep away these bugs," Stunts says.

"Toke-eeyoo, here we come," Stunts says, toasting the joint.

Cynthia approaches the mirror, hesitates.

"Take this end," Surface says, handing her the straw. "Like this, yes, uh huh, and sniff it, yes."

A line does a slow vanishing act.

"That's it. All right," Surface says.

"Go baby," Stunts says.

"Yes," Surface says. "Easy Miss Cynthia, light of my life, yes, yes. Now the other."

Things of nature around, I wake early. There's an ant, several buzzing things, a tiny scorpioid thing with too many legs, a jamboree of buzzing sounds, as on an insect preserve. In the gray of the clearing Stunts and Surface are digging a pit with sharpened sticks. Sweat spreads in broad arcs through Stunts's fatigues. Surface has the whole suit back on; the jacket's badly rumpled and frayed at the shoulders, a bit of shoulder padding peeking through; pig's blood has dried into patches of deep maroon on his shirt. I go into the woods, brambly, dotted with tinted anemones, to find a stick suitable for digging, and kick off the branch of a tree.

"You hunting for poison ivy in there?" Stunts yells.

"Give that knife here a second," I say, and when I've sharpened the stick, notched off the small branches, the three of us dig hard, loosening the dirt and scooping it out with our hands, and then, after an hour, the hole several feet deep, Surface rolls a thigh-high metal garbage can foraged on the road and we lower it, circling, until its rim rises a foot and a half above ground level, and then we pack dirt back inside it, and layers of stones.

"Got to be a low steady heat," Stunts says, half to himself.

"So you can hold your hand over it and count ten Mississippi and no more."

Behind us there is sunlight, now a faint pink from the ground and upward curling sheets of smoke. A yellow-and-black bird alights on a tree stump, twills sporadically.

"Probably a goldfinch," I say.

"Who the fuck cares," Stunts says.

Surface carries the pig from the cooler, and he and Stunts start working it across with the knife until the pig lies small and round, its two halves opposed in sharp-toothed grins, and then in quick hard motions while I hold, Stunts unlimbs it, beheads one side, lays the carcass gutted and clean on whittled sticks. We bury the innards, then start a fire in the can. I hold my hand over the flame, the heat rising slowly but surely. Like a match held way below a paper, like those milky-armed girls in Avignon. When the pain starts it widens steadily until it's a concentric pulsing through the groin. I pull away.

"That bad, eh," Stunts says.

"What?" I say.

"Your neck. The bitch has you on a short leash. You've got rope burns on your neck."

"I like the girl."

"You mean you like the bitch," he says.

"I like the girl," I say.

"She ain't bad," Surface says, humming bars of a striptease, then miming a coy undressing. "That little peep show she put on with the sheet. . . ."

"I'd consider swapping," Stunts says, socking my arm.

"Thanks, but no," I say.

"You're being just a tad territorial, Slick. What gives? You the one-at-a-time sort?"

"Yeah . . . I guess. Sometimes more than other times."

"Slick, man," he says, shaking his head. "That mono-gamey

stuff. Even the oat bran kind. That's some shit people do to mess with you 'cause they got it done to theirselves. Get with it."

"What's she, studying languages or something?" Surface says.

"Could be," I say.

"She trying to get a job at the International House of Pancakes?" Stunts says.

And he and Surface fall on the ground, rolling with laughter, Surface coughing deep, frothy spittle clinging to the side of his face.

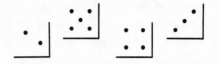

# 14

Cynthia and I soak up sunlight in a clearing, having bathed in the pond and then, her daypack stocked with water, cheese sandwiches, and Kundera, we run up an old car trail, the two of us alternately pushing the pace, until we stop in a wheat field. Insect wings flit and ignite in sunlight. We spread a towel, douse ourselves with water. Cynthia stretches and then sits and draws her T-shirt over her head. Her skin seems so wholesome against the wheat; small beads of perspiration form on her nose. I lick her nipples, sweat-salty and pink in the sun, but she pushes me away, lies down, starts bicycling her legs overhead.

"Life should be a musical," she says.

For a minute I think I should turn her upside down, shake out the cocaine. I lie, face next to hers, staring up.

"I mean," she says, leaning toward me, "people should just break out singing. There should be an orchestra—without trombones—creeping around behind us ready for accompaniment."

I nap, head on her stomach while she reads, and around mid-afternoon we walk back to the pond, whistling duets, and sit with the rest, drinking Pinot-Gris steadily, eating box after box of cheddar-flavored crackers, hunger at keen edge from the smell of the pig. And again Surface produces the vials, mirror, razor, straw, and Cynthia does a few lines right off this time, until we're grouped, powdered and silent around the smoking pig, our shadows gaunt and blurry—hardly ours—stretching and bending over the packed ground around the can.

"Awful," Cynthia says, snuffling the meat crackle, drawn, like the rest of us, by the smell. The edges of the meat are hard brown, crackling. The heat from the can rises smoky with a deep redolence, almost sweet. Surface removes the meat carefully with thick stakes and lays it dripping onto the overturned top of the cooler.

"Let's pick her," Stunts says.

"Yes," Surface says.

And Angélique is reaching, her fingers digging, recoiling a little from the heat, accommodating.

"Mmmmmmmmmm," she hums.

The smell is too rich. I want to dive my face into the pig. Become saturated in it. Angélique cracks off a crust; it crunches in her mouth. And then we are all moving in, converging on the soft middle, picking, Angélique's *incroyable mmmmmmmm* and Marcy's *oh boy oh boy* and Cynthia's *icchhhh* merge, simultaneous but distinct. I dig my fingers deep into the meat through the hot soft until I find firm layers of meat in against the viscous layers of fat, strands of tendon, steam rising around my hands, the pig grease now slick globules on everyone's hands as we squeeze off layers, clean-grained and tender, and lick our fingers. Then we're reaching again into the pig, cracking off hard and crunchy orange-brown ends, scraping the inside of the rind thick and sticky. I pick and eat, without looking up, pausing to see Stunts's intent, wordless hands working alongside mine in the grease.

"What does this stuff remind me of?" Marcy says, rubbing some along Surface's forearms, massaging it into his trapezius.

"Yes, Goddess, yes," Surface says, and soaks his hands and

moves behind Marcy, rubbing it over her waist, "Goddess, yes," rolling down the straps of her leotard and rubbing the pig grease over her breasts and shoulders.

"Thou annointest her with oil," I say, through the food buzz and the mix of highs.

"I'm being annointed?" Marcy asks, chest forward, Surface's hands sliding over her.

"Yes, Goddess, yes."

"How South Seas," Cynthia whispers to me, as if fascinated.

"Greenwich Village," I whisper back.

"Goddess," Surface says, massaging her with the grease as we eat on; "Goddess," as we strip, peel meat from the bone until the pig's near cleaned, bone showing white, and the landscape darkens; "Goddess," all of us grease-handed, stomachs full, stars sharp overhead.

We move together for the pond and work the grease off one another with the soap; I take the bar from Emma and wash around the slight smooth swell of Cynthia's waist, aroused by the publicness and wanting pure sensations right there, release from reflection, and then, without transition, eclectically clothed, we are gathered again by the pond, passing a towel, and later passing the mirror, edging straight the lines, sealing the hits with pond water up each nostril, the other blocked, and again country music wailing on.

"Yeah oh yeah," Surface yells and grabs Angélique by the waist and begins a slow cowboy waltz, dipping and spinning around the wreck of pig. "Oh baby oh" amid the fat gristle strips and strewn bones as they move into the basin of muck, ankle high, slow glide but not stumbling, suction smacks at the lifting of each bare foot.

"You're missing it, Jason. Look at this, look," Cynthia says, lying back gazing at the stars. "This is the most amazing skyscape of stars and clouds."

"I'm here," I say. "I see it."

"Do you see it?"

"Yes," I say. "Absolutely stellar."

I look up at one of those cloudscapes that shifts, revealing connect-the-dots sidereal games, the clouds not at all vaporish but collected in big sculpted forms so that, if you are a little blown away, you can see faces in it or anything else a celestial Rorschach test might dredge down. There's a thick, pasty drip back near my tonsils.

The Cadillac headlights knife across the beaten muck, where Angélique and Emma move together, dancing now and pushing each other, the beams at once illuminating parts of them and seeming about to sever, and Marcy kneels yelling "baby baby baby" as Surface looms behind her and plants two handfuls of muck on her head, rubbing them slowly down over her shoulders saying "goddess goddess goddess."

I sit beside Cynthia, wanting to draw her up beside me or to lie down with her, but she's still transfixed by the sky, body seemingly insensate. I touch the hand she rests on her stomach but she doesn't move. In the muck figures grope each other, skin gleaming in patches, forms rubbing muck on each other and embracing, almost in slow motion, huge distorted shadows dancing out over the gray fields, and I feel myself drawn toward them but stuck on the log, watching with desire, maybe ache in the blood, feeling tremendously excluded from an available great contact, part of me remembering the tightness of Emma's stomach pressing against mine at Le Cluny, and wanting to roll over and over with her tangled in a slow sloppy mud-sucking tango through muddy waves.

In among the aspens Angélique retches up several mouthfuls; her arms clutching, sliding down a tree. There's coughing, then just the music.

"Someone oughta give Marilyn Monroe a hand," Marcy says.

"Oh, she can chuck it up here," Surface says. "We all friends."

"Merde-toi, you bastard." Angélique laughs, wiping her glazed face with her arm, and moving back toward the muck, stumbling with her arms out at rightish angles as if she's doing a high-wire balancing act.

"You okay?" I call.

"*Oui,* I am okay." She waves, then calls, "Et tu, Jason. Ça va? Are you okay?"

"She's better than okay," Stunts says, resting one hand on the metal of his belt buckle. "She's about to know sweetness."

"Know what?" I say.

"Sweetness," he says. "You want a go next?"

"No thanks," I say.

"Then you might as well hold her," he says.

"No!"

"No?"

"No, Stunts," I say, getting up.

Then, looking in both directions, I realize I'm standing up and have just yelled. Angélique is bent over, hands on her knees, arms straight, her stomach moving in and out, glowering at Stunts, waiting for him. And in quick successive flashes it comes to me that I've caught myself watching a scene in which I'm present, even involved, as a spectator. I'm a spectator watching someone about to watch a man drag a woman into the muck and I must be other than a spectator. And I stand, stuck, as if poised between two mirrors, disliking what I see in either glass. I stumble forward a few steps; the motion brings a surge of dizziness, a temporary blackening at the peripheries.

"You, Stunts, you, Stunts," my voice echoes back to me. "You keep your hands off her."

Stunts shakes his head at me, opens his belt buckle and lets the ends hang, gestures me impatiently to *come on already* as he moves slowly toward Angélique, who stands with her very white arms on her hips, shaking her head and laughing. He stalks, crouching, and then charges and tackles her and brings her down face first in the muck and wrestles her, her anger and kicking brief and interspersed with strained, hurt laughter, like she's being painfully tickled, until he has her arms pinned and stretched over her head with one hand, body drawn out long, legs tangled, kissing her neck, his free hand prying her legs slowly apart.

"Hey," I say, waving my hand, and then sit down abruptly.

"Lend a pal a hand or what?" Stunts says.

"Too much," I say. "Turn her loose, Stunts."

"I beg your pardon," Stunts says, looking up from Angélique, mud rivulets tracing one illuminated cheek.

"Turn her loose."

"Why?"

"Turn her loose, I said."

"I beg your pardon?"

Stunts kisses her four, five times sloppily on the face, then licks her muddy cheek. Angélique struggles to turn but can't move, cursing and laughing, "Au secours, Jason! Jason, mon ami, mon amour, au secours!" laughing uncontrollably through her frustration, her voice at once beckoning and mockery, one arm making a beckoning gesture. Or do I just think it is?

"Is not so very funny," Angélique says to Stunts, lying very still, then struggling with a burst of energy but failing escape, until she beats the ground with her feet and lies still again.

"I beg your pardon?" Stunts says to me.

"Ease up on her," I say. "She was sick."

Surface looms up in front of me.

"Your man's out of line," I say. "He better ease up."

"Ease up shit," he says in falsetto and curtsies low to me. "Or else what? Who are you sir? Who the fuck are you, sir? Youssa, youssa, youssa. Who are you, sir?"

"Never you mind," I say.

"I's addressing you—Whitey Ford. Who are you sir?"

"Never mind," I say.

"You's Whitey Ford. Don't forget it."

I run my eyes over him, thinking action ought to be taken. He approaches in the mockery of a fighting pose, one arm rotating in a slow bolo punch. If I had to hit him I wouldn't know where to start.

"Whitey Ford, won't you come out tonight. Come out dancing. You's a debutante, you."

Nearer.

I get myself into a stance.

He curtsies again, lower, mimics my stance.

I sit back down on a log.

"Won't you come out tonight."

I look curiously at him and past him at the figures entwining in the moon-checkered clearing. Surface nods to me, all smile vanishing suddenly and spookily from his face, then a broad toothy, spreading grin. He points to me, points again, backing away slowly. Then he turns and walks back to Marcy, who shrugs over her shoulder at me, her arm hooked in his.

"I'm going to tear you up," she says to Surface, and they go off into the woods.

I see patches of Angélique's white skin now, dull ivory in the muck, wet, Stunts's camouflage shirt on her open and muddied, the suggestion of her form, her legs now around Stunts's shoulders in an improbable position, moaning combinations of *oh* and *oui* while they rock back and forth in the muck near the now-dead can, her panting finally achieving a fullness that seems to echo from speakers all around.

Then I realize that Cynthia's drawn up beside me. I feel her studying my face, but it's a minute before I can turn. She looks blown away, clothes distressed, her face lovely in dishevelment.

Each sector of her face contains a different expression: her forehead wrinkles with hurt, her eyes alternately try and sentence me, her mouth purses with aggravation.

"Did you think you were doing a grand and noble thing?" she says, glancing at Angélique and Stunts, then laughing awkward, forced laughter. She points at them where they've begun again, slowly, maybe fifteen yards off. Angélique's on top of Stunts, her white breasts now out of the shirt, the shirt sliding off one arm, her torso arching backward, her middle rotating, one hand waving and circling in the air, like she's doing rodeo.

"Go baby go baby go," Stunts says, whooping catcalls.

"Did you?" she asks.

"What?"

"Think you were being noble. Look at you. God, was that your idea of chivalry?"

"No, ma'am," I say.

"Yes it was," she says, laughing, putting her elbows on my shoulder and speaking to the side of my face. "Look at the way you're gaping at them, like the Green Knight himself."

"You're not being fair," I say, suddenly exhausted, unable to keep a sad smile off my face at the thought that it would be much nicer to roll in the mud than discuss the shoulds and shouldn'ts of other people's muddiness.

"You want to congratulate yourself for not being a pervert," she says. "But you can't take your eyes off of her. I'll bet you wish you had . . . a video camera. Just what do you think is going on out there?"

"It looks like they're fornicating," I say. "Though it's hard to tell from here."

"Why don't you sit closer?" she says, acidly. "Better yet, why don't you buy tickets and get in line?"

She walks uneasily over to where our sacks are by the pond and sits herself down in gradual stages, dropping the final foot.

• • •

I sit on a log, feeling besieged.

In the distance, Surface, Marcy, and Emma are dancing chain dances, their elbows hooked in broad square-dancish sweeps and gambols farther and farther into the fields, cutting back and forth across the now broad but diffuse headlights, as if they're following the beams. I can see their darkening figures making Rockette kicks and crazy movements out of improvisational dance, and hear patches of them all humming bars from *Eine kleine Nachtmusik*, their sounds more and more distant, bodies fainter in diffused light, my ear adjusting to hear them, and then their music out of earshot.

When I get to Cynthia she's lying on her stomach, crying softly into her hands.

"Cynthia," I say.

I take her hand. She doesn't remove her hand from mine, but sits up and dries her face with her hand. I want to kiss her hand.

"Don't you touch me."

"I won't," I say, not letting go of her hand. "I just want to hold your hand. Don't be mad."

"You don't even have any idea why I'm crying, do you?"

I have general notions but don't answer; I'm not a specialist. I loosen my hold on her hand, but don't break the contact.

"I'll know more if you talk to me," I say. "You should talk to me."

Cynthia swallows and wipes her eyes on her sleeve and rumples her hair in slow motion.

"Back there," she says, gesturing.

"Cynthia," I say. "They play by their own set of rules just like anyone else."

"So to you what they're doing back there's just the cutting edge of party games?"

"I didn't say I wanted to play."

"That was rape back there," she says.

"No."

"Rape. And you just gawked."

"It wasn't rape," I say, shaking my head. "No, no. It wasn't that."

"It was and it was like you wished you were out there wallowing with them in the mud, just like you wanted . . . what is it, a go?"

Her face is steaming underneath the faint glaze of her high, and her red hair's magnificently messy and matted on her shoulders. All I want to do is hold her, nestle my head against her chest.

"You just watched him rape her," Cynthia says, nodding as if she's convinced herself. "If you weren't going to join in or oppose or do anything you should have walked away instead of watching . . . gawking at them."

"Cynthia, I tried to do something."

"Oh, how noble of you."

"That's what they do, they play games, they act out. It's not the same as . . ."

"A man forcing himself on a woman?"

"No, not the same . . ."

But already I feel that I'm less concerned with the working out—the rightness or wrongness of my argument, whatever the lines might be drawn—than with alleviating the discomfort of not connecting, the irritation of endless scrutiny and discussion.

"They have different standards than you," I say, wearily.

"What if it had been me?" Cynthia says.

"It wasn't," I say, sharply. "And it wouldn't have been. . . . I wish you'd let me just hold you."

"I'll choose when I want someone holding me, if that's all right with you."

• • •

After two hours of shifting and rolling, I wake stiff and damp, cluster mosquito bites about my ankles. A dream has been buzzing around the edges of my sleep, the kind that's insanely paranoid when you wake.

The fields are still a dull gray-green. Cynthia's breathing swells the jean jacket I threw over her. Her feet are crusted with mud. I'd like to wake her and go somewhere high and watch the sunrise, but she's too at peace to disturb. Knowing I won't sleep again, and restless, I rise and stretch, press a few jump knuckle push-ups, and, dizzy, look around the wreck of the clearing at the hardened waves of mud where it dips around the can, the strips of pig fat, wine bottles, charred ends of sticks, dip my head into the cooler where the ice has melted, several warm DPs bob, tied episcopals. The cooler stinks vaguely of turned pig. The atmosphere of the place seems stagnant. Something catches.

Suddenly I want to see the road.

Just look at the road—stare down the laned runway of asphalt—fly away from this all.

I start through the aspens and across the field behind at a slight jog, sweating those first toxins when it's hard to tell the alka from the hol. As I run, my head clears; the landscape sharpens like a slide gradually tuned to focus. I concentrate on putting one foot in front of the other, phasing out the weariness in my legs, thinking of how Coach Black would yell at Tommy, a guy on the team who complained of tiredness midway through hill repeats. *Coach, I'm getting tired.* Coach would stand face to face with him, his whole lower face quivering with the rage of not being able to find words strong enough for his rage without cursing, finally yelling about a foot from Tommy's ear: *WELL, GET TIRED!* In the off-season Coach would turn baseball fanatic and stand, hands gripping and shaking the fence behind home plate, and cuss the umpires something fierce. *Strike, hell, you chucklehead. That wouldn't have been a strike on a worm.*

The ground between the rows is rough, and I make an effort not to trample the sweet young corn, sometimes missing and shouting strings of curses when I crush a stalk, growing stronger as I run, legs loosening, mind blanking into the concentration on short, rhythmic breaths. I could continue on into the low hills in the distance. Why stop at all? In backgammon you always get to a point where you have to decide whether to split your back checkers or block your opponent. A one-roll proposition. If you split and run one checker, the other's liable to get stuck behind a prime and smacked. You do a pip count, mental divisions. Stay if you can, depart if you must. Because after a certain distance in any internal debate, you'll talk yourself into being unhappy either way.

"It not make difference," Slav always says. "Play fast. Move, boy. If you lucky, lucky. Win, win. Lose, lose. Is fifty-fifty. If I have number I catch you one time. Then you go in the movie."

What will be the difference? My cash—still about fifteen hundred, beefed by Stunts's five hundred—is in my shoe. My passport is in my jeans. The sack is expendable. Why turn when I must find the road, the long grays and level stretchings out, gainings of speed and levelings off, setting in the stretches of nearly insane optimism, and hitch on along again, feeling the delicious solitudes? Walking, alone, a hard sausage-greasing paper in your sack, a sunset no one would believe and the selfish thrill that it's yours. You turn, then in the car, the details, the missed drop points and that sun setting, or did something slip through the translation? Find a truck driver by the road. You mount and ask *when you're done sleeping may I?* And later you're in the high seat, twisting over roads for hours in the dark, the broad avenues between banks of dark humped trees and signs looking like a lamplit trout stream.

Cynthia will be okay. Those guys, they'll just drive her to a bus. Or will they?

In the distance the bells of a church are tolling. It might be Sunday. If so the traffic will be thinner. I will get out on the road in the hard sun and choose a direction and when I get in the car I will ask the driver where he's going and whatever he answers I will smile at him with a look of surprise and joy and indicate that by happy coincidence I'm going there too. Who knows where they will wind up anyway? Every possible sequence is on the dice. Statistics are for the very long run. Keep running until you splinter bone.

And as I run into my groove, jeans starting to stick to my thighs, stride evening into a steady cadence through the haze of layered hangovers, my arms creating clear, measured triangles against my body as I lift, I remember Yakov and how after days of chess without sleeping he literally goes mad and has to be taken away. With Yakov it always depends when you play him; on the first few days no one can touch him—he plays impeccable, creative chess—but after that he plays hack level, recycling the money he's won, commenting with every hack on every move, mostly snapping *why* after every crack his opponent makes. And I run on, feeling a delicious exhaustion, that sense that when you push it, that's something, actually, however you feel the next day, a sustaining lot.

"Why?"

"Is that a move?"

"Why?"

"Stop masturbating."

"Why?"

"Because it won't come to anything."

"Why?"

"Because your queen's forked, dog."

"Why?"

"Because you have no protection."

"Why?"

"You don't need it anymore."

"Why?"

"It's getting in the way."

"Why?"

A tough question. On campus I asked an itinerant blind preacher whether God could make a stone so big even he couldn't move it.

"God wouldn't do a thing like that," the preacher said. "He isn't stupid like you are."

Why not run on?

As if every move has to lead someplace.

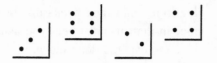

# 15

When everything seems at the expense of something else, you want range. At the first sight of the road there's always a delicious sense of aloneness. Suddenly it's just you and a strip of pavement, the gift of a blank hour, the swings, associations, raptures and ruptures that may fill it, all roads leading somewhere. I haven't felt alone, wrapped in solitude, in weeks.

A stiff breeze blows gravel along the road. The landscape composes itself. A stand of birches. A swampy, reedy low of field. The road stretches in either direction, connecting two points equally out of sight. The question is not which road to take, but which side of the road to stand on. I cross the road, then lie down and do some stretches, then sit, dust myself off. I skip stones down the road and whistle the national anthems of France, Germany, and Austria in different keys. After a time I cross back over to the other side of the road and sit down.

No traffic on the road. It's maybe ten minutes before I hear the approach of a car. I leap up and wave my hands over my head and then direct the car in for a landing with broad parallel sweeps like a runway signaler and yes the car starts slowing. It goes a hundred yards past me, ascertains that I'm not wearing leg irons, and then backs up. But when the car stops ahead of me, in that instant where you usually trot eagerly, trying not to look too eager, I don't move.

Something has a grip on me.

The driver honks twice.

Cynthia will wake, I think, feeling a tug. She'll see my stuff. She wouldn't imagine I could cut out, or would she? Maybe she'll think something's happened.

I'm standing there and suddenly just wave him on. He yells something out the window about my *mütter* and throws up his hands. When he's out of sight I rehearse my repertoire of obscene gestures after him and then, catching myself ludicrously worked up and kicking phantom objects, I sit again, laughing at my own bad theater and thinking that, like a Greek nodding his head to mean no or shaking it to mean maybe, or a Japanese waiting for the light to change at 3:00 A.M. on a barren street corner, or like some poor joker just starting in a restaurant, I need to trail behind someone, learn the moves, etiquette for a new phase, wipe the condiment trays, even the butters, marry ketchups, polish the cappuccino machine as my sensei does.

"How you play this way, boy?" Slav says, hitting his forehead with his palm. "Boy, you must to see pseeketrist. Boy, go in the movie. You mentale. How you play this way?"

"His head needs oil," Acer says.

"Why?" Yakov asks.

"Parts ain't running right."

"Why?"

"His karma ran over his dogma, Jack-off," Acer says.


From a hundred yards off I see Cynthia, seated, the shadow of a fresh dress on the beaten dirt behind her, book in hand, feet in the pond. She's mired in meditation, frowning now and then at a passage, eyes squinching. Oak trees creep nearly to the water in places and are less sharp and fine in the heat haze.

"Where the hell were you?" she asks, seeing me and putting down the book.

"Went for a run," I say.

"For three hours in your jeans?"

"I walked a bit," I say. "I was thinking."

"I hope you didn't short any circuits."

I look out across the fields from where I've come. I can faintly make out the line through the tall beaten wild grass after the cornfields, far as I can see. I take off my shoes and put my feet in the pond next to Cynthia's. We sit without talking, plunking stones into the pond. Her red hair's all disheveled. The rushes that line the banks are ringed with loam and crud from the soap and pig grease.

"So," she says. "What were you thinking about?"

"I was thinking we should take a trip."

"We're on a trip."

"Well, a different trip."

"Should we be blood brothers on it?"

"Get the knife."

When she doesn't laugh I say, "I thought about going on without you."

"But you couldn't."

"I kept thinking . . ."

"That you shouldn't leave me with these lunatics?" she says, pointing at Stunts and Surface who are headed toward us.

"Of course. But it wasn't that. Give me a chance, okay?"

"Don't give the coward a chance," Stunts says, massaging his neck. "Man does my neck hurt."

"Turn the sucker loose, Miss Cynthia," Surface says.

"Why should I give you a chance?" Cynthia says to me, as if Stunts and Surface are irrelevant.

"You shouldn't," Stunts says. "Leave the fool hanging, sugar. There's room in the Caddy with daddy."

They've each ripped off the sleeves of their garments; mud-streaked strands of padding hang frazzled from Surface's shoulders; the remnants of the suit are haphazardly ripped and mud-caked, but the handkerchief's still half-spruce in his front pocket. Their faces are mud-splotched as if they've been taking the health cure at an eczema clinic. For some reason I think of Piano Man always bragging about his cleaning bills:

"I spend a hundred bucks a week on cleaning bills," he says. "Fifty a week just on socks. I got every kind of sock. I don't never wear the same pair of socks two days in a row."

"And your feet still stink, man," Acer says, covering his nose with both hands.

"You know, I've got a mind to give you a proper licking over our little affair last night," Stunts says to me.

"Last night's over," I say.

"Is it?"

"The party's over," I say.

"Who are you to say when the party's over?" Stunts asks. He slaps a mosquito on his cheek and wipes the thin blood streak onto his neck.

"It might just be starting," Surface says.

"We may need to hunt up a mall for new clothes," Stunts says, tearing off a piece of his shirt, as if disturbed at the workmanship. "Germans do have malls, don't they, Slick? But the party's definitely not ending yet."

"It is for us. We're getting out of here."

"Why should I go any farther with you?" Cynthia says.

"I sure as hell can't figure it, Miss Cynthia," Surface says, gargling from a bottle of wine, then spitting out the wine.

"I mean, where do you get off saying 'we.' Just because we slept together a few times?"

"I just knew you guys had," Stunts says, slapping his knee. "Surf, don't say I didn't tell you so."

"Was it okay, Miss Cynthia?"

"We're here together," I say to Cynthia. "But I'd rather not talk here."

"Why not?" Cynthia says. "Do you really care what these Neanderthals think?"

"Now just hold on," Stunts says. "That's personal."

"No, I don't care what they think," I say. "What do you want me to say? What do you want?"

Cynthia stands with her hands on her hips, unable to get out whatever she wants to say. "You know what. . . . Some real . . . some. Fuck it, Jason."

I put my arms around her.

"Me too," I hear myself saying.

"Sure, Slick," Stunts says.

"Cynthia, let's just get out of here, okay?"

"Jesus, Slick. I forgot my fucking violin."

"Leave us alone, moron."

"I reckon you want that ass-whipping pretty bad, candy-ass," Stunts says, resignedly. He strips off what's left of his shirt. The fetid mess comes apart in his hand and he flings it into the trees, where it catches and hangs from a branch.

"Those sorry-ass tailors. Can't find nothing lasts anymore. Let's go, piss-pants. Time for your facial."

I motion him to lead.

"Don't be stupid, Jason," Cynthia whispers, sharply, giving Stunts a corrosive look whose force surprises me.

"What?" I ask.

"Don't fight that human muscle, he'll make a . . . a pretzel out of you. You don't have to fight him."

"I'll get some mustard," Surface says, laughing.

"You see, I wasn't giving Slick a choice," Stunts says.

"It's okay," I say, stupidly, glancing at Cynthia, who has her hands behind her head.

"What should I say?" she says, after a minute. "'Oh, be careful boys. Have a nice fight'?"

"How about a little music, Surf," Stunts says. "Make it something upbeat."

Surface salutes and walks slowly toward the car, passing Emma and Angélique, who appear arm in arm, sprigs of wildflowers in their hair, T-shirts partly torn, showing navel, like custom shirts for wanna-be bohemians.

"Bonjour, Cynthia," the girls say, almost in unison.

A blast of Jimmy Cliff's "Wonderful World with Beautiful People" springs from the ghetto blaster midway through the tape, when last call becomes rasta call.


The fight, if you want to call it that, is brief. I swing at Stunts, graze his retreating face, try to kick out his lead leg. He arm-blocks the kick, makes a low feint, and then pulls some shit-ass move out of a Judo manual, using my own weight against me. I land hard on my shoulder, and roll onto my side, looking up at him, his muscles strangely foreshortened. His foot cocks back to kick me, but he holds it suspended a second while I roll out of the way and get up, head spinning. The sun gleams on his face, making one cheek a slab of mica. The clearing seems suddenly tighter. I advance, swing at him again.

Afterwards I muse alone by the pond for a few minutes. The vees of ripples formed behind some ducks intersect to make lacework of the surface. I take off my clothes and wade out into the warm water until I'm in chest deep, the ripple spreading away from me disrupting the pattern. The water stings and soothes the bruise and slight cut on my face. A frothy algoid pond scum rings the reeds along the banks. Already I can feel a throbbing extension of my cheek, the eye closing. My shoulder aches deeply, like someone's been practicing tetanus shots on it. I find myself breathing hard, retrospective breaths, replaying but not quite seeing the means by which in a flash my arm was twisted badly behind my back, streaks of pain racing up into the shoulder socket, and my face wound up pancaked under Stunts's knee in the mud. There's still that sharp sense, almost thrill, that he's hovering over me and can snap my arm or neck, tear my shoulder out of the socket, anything else he wants with a slight twist.

"I guess you're not much of a pugilist, Slick," I hear Stunts whispering in my ear.

Oddly, no humiliation in this. Only pain and the curious sense of a sequence of mistakes and misplayed moves leading up to a position where some chronic destructionist could cut his initials on my forehead if he wanted.

"Take your stink . . . knee off my face," I say.


In the clearing the gang's sitting around the wreck of the can. Cynthia's talking with Angélique, who reclines with splendid indifference in the sun. Emma's thoroughly immersed in building a miniature farm community out of twigs. She's got a pocket knife and a pile of woods stuff she's trimming to make miniature logs.

"Le corral," she says to no one in particular. "La grange, la ferme, et la route qui quitte la ville."

Surface eyes my cheek and says, "Whitey Ford, oh my, oh my goodness."

Stunts strides up in front of me. He's still got his shirt off; there's fresh blood, presumably mine, on his face and neck.

"How you fixed for cash, candy-ass?" he says.

"Fine," I say. "I don't want to race again."

"Well, candy-ass," Stunts says, shuffling his feet and looking down. "You're not what I thought. I had hopes for you. My mistake, but a hard man is good to find, right. Anyway, I want you to have this five as a going-away present. Go on, take it, case you ever decide to get work done on your face."

"Save it and buy a new suit for yourself and Surface," I say, and drop the cash on the ground.

"Slick," he says, laughing and shaking his head. "You pick up that cash or this time I'll hog-tie you and hang you from a tree to cure in the sun."

"Buy me a good dinner with it, Herr Champ," Cynthia whispers in my ear, tugging at my elbow. "Come on. Let's get out of here before he actually hangs you from a tree."

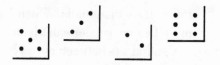

# 16

"I'd of cut you down, though, possum," Cynthia says.

Now, our second day on the road, the sun tickling the tops of trees, she's in an exceptional mood. Yesterday we walked an hour out to the road, arms hooked, barely talking. Today her face is animated, full of joy at being out on the road on a bright day. Her lows I can discount for this. After all, I think, any worthwhile person has mood-regulatory problems.

She stands with her thumb held up in the classic position, her hair fastened tight in a long ponytail. From time to time she glances at me with a bright, bemused look as if to ask if she's doing it right. I give her thumbs-up. There's a line of dirt on the side of her neck that she missed when she washed in a stream while I scoured dark pig blood off our sacks. We'd gotten a good ride into Italy and then, at nightfall, ended up bivouacking near the stream. We woke curled and rumpled together under my dew-damp, unzipped sleeping bag, light piercing through arboreal pines like a headlight.

I sit a few feet behind her with our bags, watching her and flipping through her dog-eared copy of Kundera, asking her questions about the passages she's underlined and about her rather testy marginalia. When I see the first car coming I angle myself so my gender can't be told.

Cynthia sits between me and a grandfatherly Italian business-man named Eduardo who keeps looking at us sideways with shy approval, at the way our legs brush or my hand chances to rest on the thigh of her crossed legs. When Eduardo stops for petrol he insists on springing for sodas and pastries, and while he makes a phone call, Cynthia and I share the controls on a pin-ball machine with four flippers and raining silver balls. Eduardo is going to Marseilles, which is right in line, since we're headed for Spain. But when we see the exit sign for Monte Carlo 20K, a powerful sensation wells in me, like nothing I've ever felt, the force of it almost dizzying. We drive a few kilometers in silence, the feeling growing.

"Can we get out at Monte Carlo?" I ask Cynthia, finally.

"What brainstorm now?"

"We'll rent a gown, a tux, scarf ourselves sick with that money, overlooking the Riviera. And you make all the place decisions after that."

"What is this, Jason?" Cynthia asks when we're walking the road into town, the sun now hard and bright.

"A feeling," I say.


The balcony of the Hotel el Morocco overlooks the beach where, for the past few hours, smeared with St. Tropez oil, we've been taking sun, stereotypical millionairesses promenading all around, irrelevantly clad, others sporting hooded leopard body-suit bathrobes, looking like badly out-of-season speed skaters. We swim, then walk the beach hand in hand, passing backgam-mon games. With a candy-tree flush, I watch a few antistatisti-cal moves, sheer nose guard, beach-hat suckersville, probably played for hundreds a point. Then Cynthia pulls me along.

Now, after a long hot bath together, scrubbing dirt from between toes, I sit on the balcony in my underwear watching Cynthia comb out her hair in front of a full-length mirror. Soon she'll slip into her gown; I'll run my hand along the smooth small of her back, zipping her in, then puzzle out where all my pins and cuff links go, how to get the cummerbund right to catch the crumbs. When she catches me watching her in the mirror, angling my head to get better looks, she primps up her breasts, winks.

Grubbed out on the road, you'd just as soon eat one thing as another. You salivate at the thought of a cold microwave hot dog. But when a *saucier*'s blending right you take another attitude.

The special of the day at the Maison des Poissons is bouillabaisse, chunks of red mullet, *rascasse*, jumbo shrimp, and Mediterranean fish I don't recognize—choose your *poisson*—small wedges of tomato, onion, and orange-browned, olive-oiled potatoes. The waiter sets a silver tureen and ladle over a low burner and ladles some of the brownish, piquant, garlicky sauce over our fish. There's a buttery oil and saffron sheen to the plate with its mix of chitinous shells and fish flakes in sauce. Cynthia sits across, her face suffused in candlelight, her red-gold hair, now sun-streaked blonde in places, refulgent, cascading over her shoulders, just a few traces of mosquito bites along arms.

We eat silently, hums, eye closings, losses almost of posture confirming each other's gustatory high. We eat with painstaking slowness. Dessert is hot pear tart with pear-brandy sauce. Layers of pastry and a soft inner flan coated with sugar-cinnamoned sauce. I consider ordering a half dozen to go: If you have a choice, why choose between quality and quantity?

"That was an unbelievable meal," Cynthia says. "But Jason, I'm not as dumb as I sometimes act. That feeling you had. You're here to gamble, aren't you?"

I watch the glazed pear-brandy sauce hardening on the plate.

In fact, through the pear-sauce fumes I've seen us gliding down the lamplit street toward the casino, the prospect of the tables like a low-grade fever or one more piquant, hard-to-handle sauce. We're ambling, passing through blooming mimosa and lemon trees, ostrich-feather palm leaves turning into dancer's plumes, the casino gaining ground, approaching faster and faster with a dull sweet draw, keeping me on a fine edge, conscious of the increasing presence of risk in a still unseen room where the air's different, swirling with vibes, Havana smoke. And lives, like faces, are being rearranged.

"The feeling I had wasn't about gambling when I had it," I say, thinking that, oddly, it really wasn't.

"But now you want to gamble?"

"Yes."

"You could have said so, but it's okay."

"Are you sure? I don't have to."

"But you want to."

"Yes."

We're walking along a quiet street, the air pleasant.

"Do you ever feel like gambling?" I ask.

"If by that you mean betting money, not really."

"Don't you ever just feel like dumping your purse out on the table and letting it ride?"

"My lip gloss and nail file against a two-dollar chip?"

"Why not?"

"I don't know. I mean, I've just never really liked the idea of betting money. I can see why it's exciting to other people, or to you."

"Why is that?"

"The idea of losing control. Is that it?"

"Not really losing it."

"I guess I just don't like the idea of losing money on something I don't have control over."

"You'd probably be lucky," I say.

"I might be," she says. "But there are other things I'd rather bet on."


At the sight of the Palais du Casino, which we have been gravitating vaguely toward—all roads in Monte Carlo lead to the casino as all aisles in a supermarket lead to the checkout counter—a sharp thrill rises in me, grabs at my chest. Casinos have a special sound or hum that grows louder as you approach. Sharp particulars emerge out of the hollow cool stream of air that blows from the mouth of a casino, that mouth breathing possibility. I try to muffle the sense of these things in front of Cynthia, to walk slowly, gaze around interestedly at the scenery.

"So here you are," Cynthia says, looking up. "The gambler's shrine."

I gaze up with her at the two squarish domes, the clock like a single eye, the sculpted facade. Ten o'clock. Plenty of time.

"Place looks more like a museum," Cynthia says.

"It is a museum," I say.

We skip up the stairs, into the lobby. Polished marble columns pass, our shoes echoing and clicking on a shiny black-and-white checkered marble floor. Cynthia's right, the place has a museum hush, spaciousness, coolness. We stop in a large foyer. To the left there's the Vegas-style playing room. Beyond that the Salon Privé.

"You could join me," I say, though I'm feeling a sudden pull and impatience to be alone with the tables.

"I'd rather walk around by myself for a while."

"Sure you won't mind?"

"I'll join you later, in an hour or so, okay?"

"You won't run off with any spies?"

"You'll have to chance that."

"How are my odds?"

"About like your ends?"

We kiss lightly on the lips.

"Okay, you have fun," she says.

"Do you like champagne baths?" I call after her, already feeling liberated, slipping from the sense of my own foolishness into the effervescent promise of the tables.


You stand overlooking the playing tables. A sweet, enticing voice whispers that there's no statistical law saying you can't win all night, says statistics never touch anything, says that you might just ride the wave all night, catch the glide inside the curl. Those mechanical men with the bow ties waiting behind the felt tables might keep pushing chips your way.

It's been a long time since I've gambled—scratched my forefinger along the tightly stretched felt for a card, or waved off another card, standing pat. It's been months since I walked from a casino replaying games of the night before with stinging clarity, each die depressing its dot on my memory, doing its intaglio, each card face laughing. You walk out along the boardwalk adjusting to natural light, your feet echoing hollow on the boards.

The first time I went to Atlantis was on a quadruple date freshman year in college. On the way down, jammed in the back, the guys memorized the book plays for blackjack. Straight mechanics. When to hit or stand or double-down. The girls wanted to go dancing. I knew I should defer to Deeney, my date, who I'd daydreamed of from across classrooms. I had two hundred bucks on me and went straight to the twenty-five-dollar table, figuring odds are the same, fast or slow. I'd get the gambling over with and go dancing. The dealer set three jackblacks in a row in front of me, washed the deck, and started in again. An ace, a ten. A six. Dealer busts. Unbelievable. The air around me seemed electric. Within a half hour I was up seven hundred dollars. A waitress wearing elbow-length white gloves kept bringing me double cognacs; I tossed her a ten-dollar chip. When Deeney sat next to me I bet a hundred and lost, then bet another hundred and lost. We got up. My heart was pumping. I had to fight not to turn back and bet the whole thing, instead to walk slowly toward the cashier to collect my five hundred. We went dancing and got so drunk we knocked over a line of felt stanchions. The line fell like dominoes right through the lobby of the hotel. Deeney laughed and laughed and we kissed, fumbling and then falling down on the stanchions right in front of the miffed security guards and the women lugging jumbo cardboard cups full of quarters.

After graduation, when I started counting cards and system betting, a running friend and I got stuck at the lost city for three days during which we made it a point of honor not to wire for money. Julie was in St. Croix, snorkeling with her family. We lost the limit on my friend's credit card. I pawned my watch. Lost the cash. We dozed in lobbies until moved by vacuuming clean-up crews trailing great lengths of cord. We tried hitching out for a few hours, but Atlantis is one tough place to hitch out of. We weren't in that cool, waiting mood. For an hour we bet each other on hitting a road sign with stones. We went double or nothing until we had sore elbows and wound up even. So we walked back slowly to the casino, eyeballs grazing the gutters for change, and finally hung out by the silver-dollar slot machines, getting sloshed on cognac people ordered for us, listening for the ringing and the metallic gush of coins and then asking the winner of every jackpot for a buck to help us get home. When we had enough we went to the twenty-five-dollar blackjack table and let it ride . . . and lost, again and again.

Now I am alone, in Monte Carlo, in the Salle Américaine, in a tuxedo, with money. This may have been bound to happen. Maybe it would be a crime against the gambling gods not to take a shot with what's left of Stunts's grand. I try to hold back the sensations, to walk not run to the bar for a snifter of cognac. There's that invisible hum and draw, the air all vibes that I don't want to disturb by betting. For a moment, from the bar, the casino is distant but close, like a place full of sound and smell and sight memories that I've had many times a long time ago and regard with a nostalgia at once bitter and pleasing. No specific images go through my head. Only the dull sense of having, on many previous occasions, felt this same sensation before beginning, and of having known then that, independent of whatever fortune the night might bring, at some future point I would remember having felt this way before, so that each time before I gambled I'd nod an inward greeting to those moments before and those to come.

I finish the cognac and go into a toilet stall and count the cash in my shoe. I've got two-thousand four-hundred dollars left and I convert one thousand of it into chips. The franc is at six and change. I'll need a few hundred for the plane back and a few hundred for the next weeks. I think of Cynthia out and about in that low-backed dress that doesn't quite suit her, though in a pleasant way. Cynthia flies back in two weeks and I doubt I'll want to stay much longer after she has left. If there's some spark missing with us, some lack of passion, there's also motion. Things might deepen. They already feel like they're deepening in ways I couldn't understand. We can leave Monte Carlo first thing tomorrow, head for Spain. If I lose the grand we can still go first class, room service, a sleeper on a slow train, see the Alhambra, Alcázar.

Why not?

Maybe Cynthia and I will go back together. On Granola Beach she spoke of moving to the city. Would it work? You have to know when you haven't got a chance, I used to think, before I met Julie. But maybe that's something successful people never learn.

"Hardon," Acer says. "I saw that ex of yours kissing some lard-ass in a suit."

"Let it rest, Ace."

"Near the zoo, man," he says, slapping his leg.

Say Cynthia and me were to pass her and Hallmark on a walk through the zoo. Would I enjoy Julie's slight needle-flash of jealousy at seeing me with another woman? Would I be able to act like nothing had ever happened, act like it was now clear that things had worked out for the best? Give Hallmark the old collegiate shake? What could I say to them? When you don't know what to say but feel compelled to say something you end up surprising yourself. I might apologize and wish them a happy life. After all, what could I gain by her unhappiness? But maybe it's better and more realistic to have charitable thoughts without befriending the enemy.

I tuck a thousand into the safety of my passport. No matter what, it will not come out. A good plan, I nod to my face in the mirror. It feels good to have a plan. The bathroom attendant hands me a towel, bows at the chink of my centimos on his plate.

For some reason, walking around the floor to get the feel of where I'm drawn, I end up at a roulette table. It's a game I've played only once—played without delusion of strategy—a game that's straight, brazen luck and sheikh mystique. In Europe, though, the odds are a little better, since there's only one green zero, and I figure I can buck against a two-point seven rake. After all, the casino supplies the wheel, the chips, the table, the cognac. They shine the marble, the brass banisters, the chandeliers. They deserve some edge.

I sit down at a table between an American couple in matching polyester suits with equilateral lapels and an enormous many-chinned woman who's wearing a large red fedora with a small stuffed hamster perched on its rim. She's got skyscrapers of chips in front of her. The hamster—red-eyed, downy fur—

looks so realistic that I want to ask for her taxidermist's card. A thick jeweled bracelet with a hamster traced out in garnets with crystal eyes pinches one of her thick forearms. The American couple is exuberant when they win, devastated when they lose. I watch them sweat every spin, roller-coastering with their fifty francs, asking themselves whether it's good strategy to bet this way or that, second-guessing every play, as if one play's got any more merit than another on a roulette table.

The metal partitions between the red and black numbers, the frets and canoe slots glitter against the flatter layout of the green felt, the multicolored towers of house chips, the scattered bets on numbers. The wheel head, slightly convex, glows with the mahogany of the bowl. The dealer holds the ivory ball up in against the inch-wide groove of the bowl's circumference and sets the wheel in motion, saying in his monotonous patter when it starts winding down toward its drop point, *Mesdames, Messieurs, déposez vos jetons.* Get your bets down. *Rien ne va plus.* No more bets.

The hamster woman is betting two thousand francs a shot and playing multiple three-hundred-franc numbers with fabulous unconcern, no apparent pattern to her plays. But she's winning steadily. The dealer keeps changing her chips to higher denominations; her stacks stay the same height but gradually deepen in color. The first few spins are ice, low-level, clinical, my blood acclimating to the whir of the wheel. I slide low stakes across the felt, betting the odd-even and the low numbers, feeling the low buzz of mild interest in small bets, barely the urge to look. When I win I double up, and when both ships cruise safely into the harbor and I make a small run, the chips build up and I start to feel that sense of fortune coming on. But then I slide back, slip back to even. And overall I don't really have that gambling feeling, that touch of risk, the familiar tickle along the veins.

And isn't this, after all, the idea? To play conservatively, just touch the table? Not risk anything that matters? Pay my respects, as Cynthia says, to the Gaming Gods at the shrine, kneel in the circus, look the casino square in the face like an ex–pal-clown who betrayed me but who I've now come to terms with, feel that the casino is now where I want it in my system? And then, having enjoyed a few turns with my fellow jester the wheel, I'll take my leave, wave goodbye to the ropewalkers, dwarves, freaks, tamers, kiss the terrible hand of the croupier and walk out of this place.

After about twenty minutes I start getting the urge to risk something.

It starts slowly but builds.

You look at the city of house chips built up beside the wheel. You think of the possibilities of annexing a portion of that city, shaving off a few skyscrapers, building your own penthouses. Buy Boardwalk.

If you've ever bet a hundred-a-pop hard money it's tough to enjoy a five-dollar bet, unless, of course, you have begged that five dollars at the slot machines and are trying to parlay it into bus money, or more. If you've gambled, playing for fun just isn't fun. What the hell.

I slide two hundred francs onto red. An ache has started in my chest, like a muscle pulling slowly.

The dealer sends the ball round and round, the little ball finally jumping nervously over the frets, dancing and skipping until a number reaches out and grabs it, as if magnetizing it, like there's something electromagnetically fishy and we ought to reach for a gaff. The ball rests with cool finality.

*Noir. Vingt-neuf,* the dealer says, marking the number. The croupier pays off bets and gathers in the house money, including mine, his hands flashing, moving chips around the board with fantastic precision.

I slide four hundred francs onto the red. Cynthia will be along any minute now. Why not just let it all roll a few times? The

American couple puts two hundred francs alongside mine. The man looks at me nervously and crosses his fingers. I don't respond. I'm watching the dealer prepare to send the ball rolling.

This time I'm pulling, riding with the ball around the wheel, following it with that inner chanting—come one time, just one time—that marks the entry into psychic involvement. Just one time, jump ball, one for the good guys, for the home team. Reach red. Catch 'em, snatch 'em red.

*Vert.*

A great commotion goes up for all the people who, with a truly Filipino sense of mystique, have been playing only green. The American couple looks dejected, resigned, and then they decide, nodding in tandem, to save their luck for another day. They wish me luck as they leave.

I slide eight hundred francs onto the red.

The lady with the hamster hat looks over at me, taking in the tux and the bruised cheekbone. She touches the hamster and then her chips and pushes eight thousand francs next to mine.

The wheel seems to take longer and longer. The ball slows, hangs on, then teeters and falls.

*Noir. Dix.*

Blood pounds in my ears, my stomach falls away with a sickened feeling, though I haven't moved. I've got fourteen hundred left. I move it halfway toward the layout. Split it into equal stacks, stack the chips straight, push them all onto the red. Catch 'em one time, reach for the sheltering dunes on the beach just once.

Without looking at me this time the woman touches her hat, takes the top chip in her stack and rubs it against her bracelet, then turns it over, and slides fourteen thousand francs onto the red next to mine. The croupier says something to the pit boss who nods and writes something on a notepad. Intimidation move. Offer her a credit line. Irritation mess-with-your-rhythm gorilla tactics. The woman doesn't move. Odd shadows, caused by the multiple light sources, play over the table.

First the ball circles the track and I concentrate my psychic energy on willing it to drop into a red slot. Then the wheel seems to slide around the ball that hovers, like it's losing its grip, like it's fastened by pitons about to pull loose from the rim of the wheel and send it on a flounce-jounce-dance along the wheel walls. The wheel has slowed. Numbers become clear between the gleaming frets. Red fingers reach against black as in competition fungo, straining after the small ivory ball, the white ball dropping, skipping, plunking in red, popping out, into black, popping out again, until a fret lunges out, grabs, and, still circling, as if pinned on the rim of a vortex, fastens it with that arresting, seemingly bunkoed suddenness.

I lean forward to look.

*Noir. Trente-et-un.*

Hamster doesn't look at me or flinch. I get up, a little dazed and wobbly, like when you go to the john after five quick whiskeys. My head spins, faces an odd blotch of flaming and freezing spots. She slides another stack of chips onto the red. I stand a few paces back. The ball drops into red.

*Rouge. Neuf.*

Hamster lets it ride.

*Rouge. Vingt-cinq.*

I go to the bar to order a cognac.

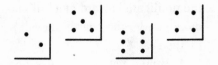

# 17

Sipping Courvoisier makes many things immediately better. Often after a hammering at backgammon there's even a delicious melancholy in sitting with one's elbows on the wood bar, the rage draining into the problem of how many drinks you can now afford, rate of consumption equaling amount of cash divided by time, and all of it—that you're doomed to drink your solution, stop at your quotient—seeming suddenly one more ridiculous fact in a ridiculous night so that you laugh aloud, ridiculously, and people at the bar eyeball you with Mount Rushmore sympathy. As if, wall-eyed stonily beside you, cigarette butts in their previous drink, they're any better off.

But now the question remains of what to do next. I've just lost a thousand dollars. A grand fact. Another casino casualty. Like when you sit in Atlantis and watch some Chinese guy, Boy Scout troop leader, or rabbi lose five grand in ten minutes at a five-dollar table and then walk off, having hardly touched the rhythm of the table, and you never wonder if he's going home, whether that was the last critical play that he'd been working up to for ten years, the proceeds of years of shining every grape outside his Oriental grocery, robbing cerebral palsey boxes, or if he's the profligate bastard of a billionaire recluse, or has a gun in his mouth under the boardwalk, all peaches and cream, going down by the sea.

A woman catches my eye and nods, holds her head to one side in a questioning way like a bird or someone with water in her ear. She's wearing a paisley dress with a top indistinguishable from lingerie and a wide-rimmed hat that looks like a placemat with a plasticated airline dinner on it. I nod back, raise my snifter to her, look back over the casino. Configurations of players huddle together under the lights, the lights highlighting slabs and angles of their faces.

The casino is strangely muted, only occasional murmurs, the whirling sound of the wheel, the ball bouncing, the croupier's patter, an occasional slot ring, all very still in comparison to Atlantis, where garish carpeting assaults the eye, and there's always a slot ringing, a hot craps table riding every roll, a bar band belting rock—Atlantis, where cigar smoke hovers in the lights over the tables until the long night ends, like others, your throat dry, mucus stripped away. And if you've lost, you shuffle out onto the boardwalk staring curiously at molting pigeons fighting over trash, Kansans in checkered jackets photographing the ocean, the sky just gray behind the enormous billboards, air nonetheless marvelously fresh. And you sit on a bench washed out and dizzy-feverish and pocket empty and full of the forced and circling but still remote self-fucking examination beatings bring.

Suddenly, I burn with a sense of my own foolishness. Blood rushes to my face, like I'm in the window of a Madison Avenue clothier trying on silk pajamas that don't fit. If only I had quit. With that money, the equivalent of some starving village's annual product, we could have stayed here in style for three days. And eaten a whole village's annual product in sushi or nouveau shrimp vindaloo? Wouldn't that have been worse? A moment's reflection tells me I don't mean any anger toward myself, and that if I cared in any meaningful way about starving villages I'd be off organizing grain shipments.

Mostly there's the question, the topic my mind won't leave. There's the slow, electric hum and draw, steady and persistent, of the question. Can I quit when I still have a thousand dollars in my pocket with which to get even, maybe even win, start a streak that no statistical law says ever has to end?

Isn't there something to be said for standing ready in a sensible way to play the fool, for letting it ride the extra time or two? Win or bust? Double down or nothing?

That I have a thousand dollars left in my passport is also a fact. Can I refuse risking another pop for stakes that matter? How many opportunities come up where you can muck everything up or score? I consider changing five hundred more and just placing it on the red. If I do and lose I'll definitely have to leave. There will be inconvenience, as there generally is, but I will have settled things, achieved temporary clarity. This night will end and another one will follow it, whatever the terms, whether I'm sleeping in the bus station, begging bits of baguette, shaking a cup for francs, or scattering francs among bellboys along the Riviera.

You always know, if you go broke you can go to a bar where there's live music, walk around passing your hat, then skedaddle, motor out of there, man, motor. You can cut the flowers out of someone's garden and sell them to motorists at stoplights. You can join the wrecks who forage the garbage cans of the rich for objects to sell the middle class. Collect bottle caps around City Hall at lunch hour.

No chances, no romances.

So I ask myself, What would Dostoevsky do in my position?

•   •   •

Once a play has begun you must complete it. If you bet on a pony and then back off at the last moment, that pony tramples the track record every time.

I change seven hundred dollars, pocket thirty-five hundred francs in chips.

Then I take the chips out and look at them. They're nicely engraved, glorified poker chips. So light and smooth. Something to drill a hole in and hang from your ear.

I walk around the casino, shuffling chips between my fingers, and find an open seat at a roulette table and sit down without looking to either side. The thing to do is bet it all. I watch the wheel for two spins, both black. The odds don't change because you make a hundred little bets rather than one big one.

I still haven't seen anything but the wheel. I'm holding thirty-five hundred francs' worth of chips. The croupier calls out for bets.

I station the whole stack on the red.

The wheel starts spinning, speeds into a blur, the wheel whirring cleanly, red and black spokes ticking and slowing into more distinct ticks, like the wheel's just been trued, my eyes willing the whirl through its phases of motion, my hands resting on the table, relaxed, detached things.

I sit straight, not taking my eyes from the wheel, but somehow in that gray becalmed zone, out of consequences, suspended, waiting to see from which direction the sails fill, winds waft. The ball dives, leaps like spray, plunges again. Sticks.

*Rouge.*

I leave my bet on red, not touching the original stake, raking the house chips in.

*Rouge.*

Don't double, I say to myself. Hold back. Don't do it yet. Remember Sammy's backgammon axiom that timing equals freedom or greater chances for movement. Feel that streak first, that widening glint of a redemptive swing into parlay. *Parlay vous red.* Maintenant. Catch 'em, snatch 'em. Again and again, like you own and recharge the magnet.

*Rouge.*

And suddenly I'm out in a clearing. The trees open out. It's a moonlit night, pinpoints of stars, the mossy overgrowth of a tropical rain forest, all crackling, the sound of the sun drying blowdown like cereal claiming milk. I'm back. A sustained, muted, vague exultation. The road stretches out, offering relief and escape, movement, that movement through landscapes in the dark without being moved, gadding about and a kind of stillness at the core. As if I never should have lost the faith, as if anything had ever mattered enough to make my heart beat the way it just beat, and beats still.

Now double up, I think. With the house's money, the interest on a gift. Or quit now, walk on by. Now that you're clear, survived the kill, the wheel lifting you off and away with the whirring of helicopter wings.

*Noir.*

I bet again.

*Noir.*

Okay, okay. In good time.

*Rouge.*

Now double up, press your bet, stack them. I stack the chips and slide them forward.

*Noir.*

Too soon. Back to basics. I slide out the thirty-five hundred.


I've got back my original grand and am up seven thousand francs when Cynthia puts her hands on my shoulders. The touch startles. At first I don't think who it is, how long she's been there, how many spins I've taken. Hours might have passed.

"You look like such a gambler in that outfit," she says. "The way you push the chips out, so serious."

"We both look like we're cut from a cognac ad," I say.

The wheel is about to spin.

*Mesdames, Messieurs, déposez vos jetons.*

"You haven't been bored, have you?" Cynthia whispers, jokingly.

The dealer's hand is on the wheel. The wheel starts to turn slowly, readying.

*Rien ne va plus.*

"What?" I say. "No. Where'd you go?"

"I wandered around."

I look up at her from the seat. She smiles, crosses her fingers, gives a hopeful, encouraging expression that wraps me, makes me flushed, disconcerted, giddy all at once, like a sudden, disabling panic attack.

The wheel spins off, glinting, making its fast then slowing spoke sounds. Tick-tick-tick-tick, tick-tick, tick.

*Rouge.*

Without looking up again I stack the chips, double down, head ringing. Cynthia's got her hand on my neck, fingers under the shirt collar.

"You doing okay?" she asks.

"Yes," I say.

And suddenly I want out of the casino, feel claustrophobic, hemmed in and burning, just want to be gone. I'm ready to dash for the door, but pinned to my seat, like a bad dream you know you're cased in but can't bust out of. And just as the dealer rubs the white ball up against the runway of the wheel, caressing the wood with it, begins *Rien ne va plusing* us, I reach out and lift my thirty-five hundred off the red, spring up. The croupier shoots me an annoyed look.

I pocket the chips, dropping him a fifty-franc chip. His assured look says, *Congratulations, but we'll meet another time,* and maybe we will, but not tonight.

"Let's go," I say, hearing the wheel spinning behind me, ball bouncing with its uneven clicks against the even ticking, about to find its exact slot, its place in the grand sweep of things, which, I think, it is better that I not know now.

"Wait, wait. There's no rush," Cynthia says. "I liked watching the game. Watching the people's faces, the way everyone's eyes follow the ball."

"I've had enough," I say, heading straight for the cashier, still feeling the croupier's look pressing against my back.

"Wait, Jason. What's the rush?"

"It's stuffy in here."

"Stuffy, come on. You wanted to play, so play."

"I played."

"But I wouldn't mind watching a little," she says.

"Another time," I say.

"But I'd like to. What if . . . I want to bet my lip gloss? What about that?"

"Please," I say. "Tomorrow, maybe. If you like. I want some air."

Cynthia hooks her arm in mine.

"Cheezus," she says, slowing me down, shaking her head. "Relax, Champ. These shoes weren't made for casino racing."

"Take them off then," I whisper.

The cashier counts and recounts the large franc notes, bids us good evening.

"What is it? What's wrong? Just tell me," Cynthia says in a mock-weary tone when we're outside. She sets her shoes on the edge of the terrace.

My mind's racing. Round and round. Red. Black. Red. Black. Green. Zero. It's like I've escaped something, the door's slammed shut behind me. When they bust it down they won't catch me. I'll be hurdling beams of sunlight, basking in shadows.

"Nothing's wrong," I say, breathing deeply.

"Tell me what it is."

"Sometimes you just want air."

"Did you have fun, Mister gambler?"

"Yes. I had fun. How about you?"

"Yes."

"Where did you go when you wandered?"

"Around," she says, circling her finger in the air like a swizzle stick. "That cash you just got. Did you win all that?"

"Some of it."

"Really."

"You must have brought me luck."

"Are we going to bathe in champagne?"

"What year?"

"You actually won?"

"Why shouldn't I?"

"No reason."

"Well, I did."

"That's fantastic. Aren't you happy?"

"I'm happy."

"Then act happy."

"Okay," I say, facing out over the dark sea so she won't notice how my face burns.

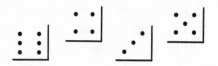

# 18

We're sitting by the water, the sky now faintly blue and gray, sunrise maybe two hours off. The outlines of yachts form on the horizon, gamblers cruising out past the limit. If you concentrate into the stillness you think you hear suggestions of sporadic laughter. Just out of range. Cynthia's asleep; she shifts upward against my shoulder. I'll wake her for the sunrise, a coffee-ad move.

I take off my white bow tie, undo the first few buttons on my shirt, and clip the bow tie to my coat lapel. I massage my bad ankle, stiff from walking around in the hard-soled shoes. The beach stretches a few hundred yards back toward the lights of the casino and the hotels nestled against the cliffs where cool blank squares suggest terraced gardens. Somewhere in the gray there are the parallel prints of our bare feet, stretching by the water, tracks partly erased by the refluent tides, but still ducking in and out of sight, reappearing like ribbons in the sand our feet must retrace. That dinner tastes in my mouth, but I've got a raging appetite—and cash. Why not order up some deviled eggs and dance to the silver notes of glass chiming against glass over a flute of champagne?

A man with a metal detector works his way toward us. He has a flashlight attached to the sensor, and a utility flashlight clipped to his waist. He passes a few feet from me without waving. I watch him, the level sweep and swing like he's vacuuming, the way he hesitates, checking every lead. The beams spray away from him at different angles as he sweeps back and forth over the sand. When the metal detector beeps he brushes the area, brings both beams to bear on the source of the beep, probing, combing among butts, corks, bottle caps for someone's long-lost ruby earring.

Cynthia's breath is gentle on my face. I look at her and then out at the dark sea and sit there thinking that right now I really am a thoughtful young man. I poke her face lightly and she doesn't move. It would be a feat to slip my fingers into hers without waking her. When my pinkie hooks hers she mumbles "totalidiot," smiles faintly, squinching her eyebrows together. So she's either awake or dreaming of someone else.

And suddenly I'm remembering that first night in her Paris hotel, the angle of her head leaning out of the bathroom to ask whether I was just going to walk around with stinky water all over me, and later, after a steaming shower the stillness of our breath returning, the way when we'd caught our breath and gone back into the bedroom we lay with bars of light from a sign slicing over our tangled feet, and the way that even at that time I was remembering how, as we walked up the steps of her hotel I'd been thinking, aware of the distance of the thought, that she might just be proving she was game, and how I almost wished— shivering half from cold in the center of her room while I rubbed warmth into my chicken-skin arms with a towel and fished in my sack for something passably clean, a pair of dry drawers— that there were a way to exit gracefully, slide down a greased fire escape, preserve the ache of pursuit.

Maybe stateside, if she's interested, we'll look for a place together, join monies? If you try figuring things step by step on your own, you're exhausted by the time you reach base camp. When I get to the House of Backgammon I'll consult Sammy and Acer.

"Hey," Sammy will say, scanning for sloppiness, holes in the play. "Hey kid, it's a move."

And if it's a bad move? Well, maybe it's worse to go through life without exposing your face to the knife, committing suicide a few times.

"Don't tell him," Acer will say. "And, Hardon, mental klutzes like you shouldn't be in Monte Carlo."

"Why?" Yakov says.

If I had connections I'd build Yakov a statue, have his face put on a First Day of Issue or sculpted into the side of a mountain or engraved on a bill. I'd get a day named after him.

"If you like, you like," Slav babbles. "It not make difference. Sometimes lucky. If you lucky, lucky. If you no have luck, you must to go in the movie. What you scared from?"

"Don't educate the fish," Acer says.

"Why?"

"Enough of that *why* business, already, Jack-off. It's good for him to pay."

"Why?"

"You haf to hilp him," Slav says, face red and intent. "You must to teach this good boy how you play."

"Why?"

"Come on, Ace," I say. "We're all in this fucking bouillabaisse together."

"Okay, Hardon. Follow the words of the Buddha."

"Why?"

"It is the path of wisdom."

"Wisdom?"

"Hardon, you witless cretin. You learn anything yet?"

"Not much, Ace."

"Hardon, you got to stop eating soup with a fork. Wipe that

crusty shit out of your eyes with Q-Tips, man. There's knowledge everywhere."

"You mean there's smoke everywhere," Sammy says. "One of you turtleheads open a window."

"And then jump out of it," Yakov says.